Matchmaking the Cowboy

A SMALL-TOWN CHRISTIAN ROMANCE

CHRISTMAS IN REDEMPTION RIDGE

EMILY CONRAD

Chapter One

"You are not Dr. Carter." Hollis fought the urge to cross his arms and stand like a barricade at the entrance to the Price Quarter Horses stable. Family was everything, and aside from his mom, who lived at and worked the ranch with him, nothing represented what remained of his family more than the business he had inherited from his father—troubled though it was.

His usual vet, the one Dad had trusted for decades, was an older guy vaguely reminiscent of a pug.

This woman had an edge on Dr. Carter in that respect. Willowy with big eyes and a little upturned nose, she looked like a cartoon princess dressed down to blend in with the commoners, cowboy hat and all. She extended a slim hand. "Lucy Aveline. My clients call me Dr. Lucy."

"Hollis Price." He suspected she'd known his name just as he'd known hers. Redemption Ridge was a small town, and they'd both grown up here. He'd seen her at church every week since he'd moved back almost two years ago.

What he hadn't known until her fingers closed around his palm was that her dainty hands boasted a firm grip. But firm enough to indicate she had the strength required to be a large animal veterinarian? Besides, she'd been about five years behind him in school. That made her thirty or thirty-one. She couldn't have finished vet school more than a handful of years ago.

"This is my assistant, Chantal." Her breath puffed white in the December air as she motioned to the passenger side of the vehicle.

The shorter, younger woman waved and beamed at him. Hadn't seen a grin that big pointed in his direction since he'd quit the rodeo.

Dr. Lucy's full lips remained lifted in a smile that was more courteous than adoring. "As for Dr. Carter, his wife is sick today, and he needed to stay with her. He didn't want to reschedule the gastroscopy since Pepperjack has been fasting for it." She quirked an eyebrow. "He *has* been fasting, right? Sixteen hours from food and two since his last drink?"

"Yes, ma'am." Dr. Carter would've known better than to question his ability to follow simple instructions when the health of one of his horses—this horse, in particular—was on the line. Then again, Dr. Carter also should've known Hollis wanted only the best care for Pepperjack, yet he'd sent someone less experienced? A sense of betrayal mixed with the concern already bubbling in his gut.

"Then let's get going so the poor guy can eat." She flounced to the back of her truck and lugged out a supply kit large enough that she could probably curl up inside.

Hollis moved in to help. Too slowly, apparently, because Lucy—pardon, *Dr.* Lucy—already had it on the ground.

She snapped the handle in place to roll the tote like a suitcase. "I looked over the notes, but tell me about his symptoms."

The symptoms. The one reason he couldn't send Dr. Lucy away in favor of waiting for his usual veterinarian. "He's the spryest twenty-nine-year-old horse I've known, but in the last two weeks, he's slowed down on trail rides and lost his appetite. Grinding his teeth some, lying down more often. Dr. Carter suspects stomach ulcers."

"Don't you worry." Chantal appeared at his elbow, most of her teeth showing through her ongoing grin. What looked to be a laptop bag hung from one shoulder. Her other hand held a black canvas case. "Ulcers are treatable and don't often turn serious—except in foals, of course, which is basically the opposite of Pepperjack."

If Pepperjack was the opposite of a foal, that meant his time was coming sooner than later. Hollis's chest constricted as if one of the horses had pinned him against a wall. Pep had been a member of the family since he'd been born in a stall just feet from where they stood.

"Quarter Horses can live to thirty-five or even older." If Dr. Lucy spoke because she noticed his distress, she didn't show it as she scanned the snow-dusted riding arena, pens, and pastures that stretched outward from the stable. "No reason to think you don't have plenty of good years left with him."

Hollis had grown up around horses. He knew these things. Yet at the reassurance, his lungs began to function again. He followed her survey of his property. Tucked into the mountains of Colorado's Western Slope, his family had lived and worked on this land for generations. Used to be they kept some cattle, in addition to the horses, but Dad had narrowed the focus. Now, the ranch bred, raised, and trained Quarter Horses. Dad had made a name for producing some of the best ranching and roping horses in the country.

A name that was up to Hollis to carry on, starting with taking the best possible care of one of their first champions, Pepperjack. He exhaled slowly, telling himself for the hundredth time that Pep would, as both ladies had said, be fine.

Hollis extended his hand for the case the assistant carried. "I can get that."

"Oh, thanks." She passed him the handle. He'd barely hooked his fingers underneath when she also slung him the laptop bag. Then her hand landed on his chest. "You're so chivalrous."

He shifted back, and her fingers dropped from his canvas jacket.

The wheels of Dr. Lucy's kit bumped over the lip at the threshold of the stable. "Chantal, would you mind hanging back and calling ahead to Bertie? We're going to be running behind, so it'd be helpful if she already had the halters on the alpacas when we got there."

The assistant deflated and retreated toward the passenger seat of the truck.

Hollis dipped his chin to Dr. Lucy. She'd saved him twice in two minutes. She was no Dr. Carter, but someone this observant and considerate would tune in to the needs of the animals in her care. Maybe she could handle a routine stomach scope. He led her deeper into the stable.

She fell in step beside him and dropped her voice. "I had a talk with her on the way out, but she went to watch you in the rodeo finals two years ago because she'd heard you were retiring. Instead of giving her closure, I think she came home from Vegas an even bigger fan. If I remember her raving correctly, you and your brother took the team roping championship, and you set a new average time record in calf roping?"

It shouldn't bother him that she spoke as if she had only secondhand information. Why would she respect him for his career when he'd been so leery of her in hers? And yet, he found himself wanting to win her over. "Not a fan yourself?"

"Work keeps me pretty busy, but one can't help hearing things in Redemption Ridge. Especially between Chantal and your dad. He was so proud, he told everyone he saw."

Since Dad's death in February, Hollis felt like he lived in a booby-trapped house, never sure when the floor would give way beneath him and drop him into the cold, dark cellar of grief. Physically, he continued toward Pepperjack's stall. Emotionally, Lucy's statement sent him tumbling. Should have known better than to fish for compliments. He caught the last shreds of his composure and held on for dear life. "Pep's stall is just ahead."

The indoor riding arena took up the center of the building. Arranged in a U, the stalls surrounded it. Pepperjack's was at the very tip, farthest from the main entrance and across from the office.

He looked over his shoulder. Frank, his righthand man and the ranch's only non-family full-time employee, led a horse back to its stall, but there was no sign of Chantal. "I didn't think to tell your assistant where to find us."

"I'll text her. Bertie's a talker, so she'll be a few minutes yet. Should give me time for the initial exam." She pecked at her phone.

Hollis unlatched and rolled back the stall door. He collected Pep's halter from the hook as the gray gelding zoomed forward to check his pockets. Over time, the horse's dapples had all but faded, leaving him with a speckled white coat best described as flea-bitten. Mom enjoyed baking, and Hollis rarely stepped in a stall without a pocket full of homemade treats. Pepperjack could probably smell the apple-and-oat cookies he'd given to some of the others that morning. Finding none for himself, the horse nosed Hollis's hat from his head. Hollis caught it by the brim and settled it back into place.

Dr. Lucy lifted her eyebrows.

"I told you he was hungry." He fit the halter on Pepperjack and held him back from frisking the doctor.

"And he has reason to expect something in your pockets?"

He didn't bother hiding his smile. The horse deserved to be spoiled in his golden years.

By the time he hooked a lead to the halter, Dr. Lucy had her stethoscope looped behind her neck. She started the exam. Pep leveraged the proximity to pat her down for goodies. When he again came up empty, he nudged the brim of her hat and flipped it to the ground with a low whinny.

Lucy coughed a surprised laugh as her long, brown hair slipped forward to softly frame her face. Though he believed her to be as strong as her job demanded—and large animal vets did need strength—something about her sparked his protective instincts. She really was pretty, but this loyalty stemmed from something more. The gentle way she interacted with him, perhaps.

"He does that every time he doesn't get a treat?" she asked.

"Seems he had reason to believe you'd have a treat for him too." Smirking, he swept up her hat and dusted it against his jeans to clear it of wood shavings.

Lucy chuckled as she accepted it back. "I suspect he does, but that has nothing to do with me." Hat in place, she stroked Pep's forehead, and her tone turned gooey. "Have you been spoiled? Or maybe it's your just deserts after all the championships and awards."

Pep snorted with indignant agreement.

She paused the stream of sweet talk to listen for a pulse, then picked it up again. "Horse of the Year a couple of times, competed in at least, what, four world championships?"

She was probably talking more to the horse than to him, but he answered anyway. "Competed in ten. Won something in six."

Pepperjack swiveled his head toward Lucy.

She seemed to take it as a request that she continue the story of his glory days. "Six wins, buddy? Would that be once with William Price Senior and five times with this guy? Tell me, Mr. Pepperjack, do you still have to fight off female attention too?"

Pep tossed his head right on cue.

Hollis fiddled with the lead. He'd wanted his past to impress her, and in a roundabout way, praising Pepperjack like this did indicate a certain respect for Hollis. But this was weird, right? Her talking to the horse about female attention, and Pepperjack somehow egging her on? Except Hollis regularly wandered the grounds, talking to his late father, asking all the questions he wished Dad could answer. Maybe he was in no position to judge.

Footsteps in the aisle meant the assistant had caught up. Thankfully, she focused on preparing the endoscope, and Dr. Lucy turned her attention to questions about Pepperjack's health history. Afterward, she administered a light sedative.

As it set in, Pepperjack's head lowered, and his alert gaze turned sleepy. Hollis clenched his jaw and averted his gaze.

Routine. This was routine.

Still, he knew how it went with animals. One of Pep's last experiences would likely be an injection that would set in not unlike this. Hollis dragged his fingers over his cheek and willed the thought away. This day was not that day.

Today, most likely, they'd find only what they expected: ulcers. Still, worry niggled in his chest. They might find something worse. Or perhaps the scope would reveal only healthy tissue, and the diagnosis would be that Pepperjack was finally showing his age and slowing down. Hollis wasn't ready to see Dad's horse decline. Not as he headed into his first Christmas without the man.

"I think he's ready." Dr. Lucy drew near with the endoscope.

Roused by the tube going up his nose, Pepperjack nodded against Hollis's grip. The sign of his strong spirit bolstered

Hollis. He held Pep steady as Dr. Lucy guided the tube into place.

A mostly pink image appeared on screen. The assistant moved in and held the scope still as Dr. Lucy worked the controls and watched the live feed of Pepperjack's stomach.

A ridge of yellow bumps appeared in the otherwise pink picture. "Looks like we have some Grade 1 ulcers."

"That's the least severe." The assistant angled her head toward Hollis but had the sense to keep her line of sight trained on his horse.

Dr. Lucy motioned at the screen. "The yellow means the stomach lining has been damaged, but the mucosa is still intact. We'll treat it with omeprazole. Usually, that resolves it within four weeks, but I'll let Dr. Carter's team know to schedule a recheck at that point so you can be sure Pepperjack's good to go."

Ulcers. As expected. Four weeks of treatment meant he'd need that recheck right between Christmas and New Year's. Hollis nodded his agreement with the treatment plan, yet his relief struggled to overcome the melancholy inspired by seeing Pep like this.

As she removed the scope, Dr. Lucy outlined feeding strategies. He knew the drill, but the way she rattled off the information, these were the routine facts she reminded everybody of when they got this diagnosis. He'd worried about her inexperience, but she knew her stuff.

"Any other questions for us?" Lucy was back in the hall, her hand on the handle of her kit.

The assistant raised her eyebrows and bit her lip, like a question from him would be a coveted prize.

He shook his head once. "I can take it from here. Thanks for stepping in."

"Of course. Nice meeting you, Hollis." Dr. Lucy extended her hand again.

He shook it, then nodded to the assistant. "You too. Have a nice day."

Perhaps he ought to show them out, but he couldn't stand to leave Pepperjack. Still sleepy from the sedative, the horse shifted one foot and stared lazily at the wall, a shadow of his usual self. He'd be back to normal within the hour, healthy by Christmas.

Still, horses didn't live forever, and it didn't matter which vet he worked with. None of them could hold off the inevitable forever. Sooner or later, Hollis would have to figure out how to survive another loss when he wasn't sure he or the ranch would recover from the last one.

Chapter Two

Lucy tapped her fingers on the steering wheel as she drove through Redemption Ridge toward Bertie's Alpaca Farm. Should she say more to Chantal about professionalism? Or had that extra task of calling the ever-chatty Bertie been enough of a consequence?

It wasn't as if Lucy could entirely blame her. Chantal had eyes, after all. Hollis had handsomely sharp features that softened when he smiled and a build strengthened by the physical nature of ranch life. And the man's attachment to his horse? Enough to make any animal-loving woman weak in the knees.

"Can we stop at Donut Haven for coffee?" Chantal asked.

The black awning protruded from a brick storefront one block up, crowded between other downtown businesses. Lucy wouldn't mind an extra dose of caffeine and warmth herself, but the extra stop at Price Quarter Horses had put them behind. Bertie's long-winded stories would likely strain the schedule even more. "Sorry, but I don't think we can swing it today unless we manage to wrap up with the alpacas by ten."

Chantal sighed.

Even Lucy couldn't help a glance at the business as they

passed. With all the parking spaces in front of the building occupied, they'd have to pull around to the lot in back, which would add even more time to the stop. Definitely couldn't—

Wait.

The license plate on one of the vehicles read *Doc C*.

If Dr. Carter's wife was so sick, why had he ventured out for coffee or donuts? The vehicle's door swung open, and out popped the gray-and-brown bob cut belonging not to Jack Carter, but his wife, Dolores. With energy that suggested Dolores was not only well, she was downright chipper, she waved to Margie Buchanan, who advanced up the sidewalk.

Lucy flipped on her blinker and swung around the corner, headed for the back parking lot.

"What's going on?" Chantal clutched the armrest as if trying to stay on a bull.

"Change of plans. We're getting coffee after all."

Dr. Carter had some explaining to do, but before she confronted him, Lucy was going to do a little reconnaissance by talking with his wife.

Or at least, that was the plan until she reached the parking lot and saw the huge black pickup parked prominently near the rear entrance. Her breath left her, and her foot reflexively mashed the brakes.

Chantal squawked, and her head swung toward Lucy and then toward the truck. "Oh." A beat of silence. "You know, we *are* late, and Bertie always means well. I don't like having to cut her off if we have time."

Lucy bit her tongue. She shouldn't have to cower and hide from her ex. She hated that was her instinct. Yet, she shifted into reverse and backed onto the street. She already had to see him far more than she wanted, and every time she felt belittled and controlled.

There was a Bible verse about not having a spirit of fear,

but one of power instead. What would that look like? Breaking her ex's manipulative rules, perhaps?

Her pulse pounded at the thought. Could she do that? Defy him?

Not outright, but technically he'd never said she *had* to ask to stop by his ranch to see Rosie and Jasmine. It just seemed to Lucy like the proper way to do things, so she'd always cleared her visits with him. But he wasn't treating her properly. She shouldn't have to return the favor. She needed to take back her power.

So, after a solo stop at a nearby farm that afternoon, she pulled into Drake Hasting's drive.

Her breath stuttered in time with her galloping heart, but the stately brick home showed no signs of movement. He might still be in Redemption Ridge or back at his own office in another nearby town. Her gaze swung toward the barn, a brick-and-wood structure fancy enough to pass as a house itself. No sign of any people there either.

She reached into the grocery bag of goodies she kept on hand for the animals she treated. She collected some carrot tops and apples, then hopped from the truck, eyes on the nearest fence. Usually, Rosie and Jasmine met her there, but today, neither one peered out.

She let herself into their paddock. A trough, hay, and piles of cow manure all attested to what she ought to find there, but the animals weren't present. Oh, but the gate at the back of the enclosure was open.

Lucy jogged across the distance. The small paddock opened into a larger pasture that Drake must've been using for beef cattle, given the corn feeder. A full-time lawyer, Drake also maintained a hobby ranch. Thanks to trees and a dip in the land, she couldn't tell exactly how far to the right the pasture extended or whether the distant cattle had access, but thankfully, the only cows in sight were two small, familiar ones.

They lingered near a fence shared with another enclosure, where a distinctive gray-and-black horse grazed. Though Drake had originally prized the horse because of his rare grullo coloring, Ovation had been relegated to that field before Lucy had ever dated Drake. The only time she'd seen the horse outside of it was in a video Drake had posted. In the clip, Ovation threw Drake and then refused to let him mount again. When cornered, the horse bit him. The caption blamed Ovation's trainer, none other than Hollis Price, for the behavior.

During her relationship with Drake, she'd figured the truth was somewhere in the middle. That Hollis had made some mistakes, but that perhaps Ovation had come to Price Quarter Horses with issues Hollis simply wasn't prepared to handle.

These days, she knew better. Not only had Hollis been adorably attentive with Pepperjack that morning, but she'd experienced Drake's ugly side for herself. She'd also met Nora St. Clair, whose family had sold Ovation to Drake. She swore the horse was sweet-tempered. The facts pointed to Drake alone causing Ovation's aggression.

Turning him out in the field and leaving him alone was the best thing Drake could've done for the horse, and she felt a little bad stealing Ovation's company, since he grazed near the fence almost as if he enjoyed the cows' presence.

But Rosie and Jasmine spotted her, and the two headed toward her as fast as their short legs would carry them. The miniature Highland cattle had fluffy coats and horns that extended about as far as their ears. Rosie was the traditional copper color, while Jasmine's white coat contrasted with her black nose, ears, and hooves.

Lucy had fallen in love the moment she'd seen them, and

the one-third-sized cattle had fallen for her too. Theirs was a star-crossed love story, thanks to Drake, but at the moment, the pair reveled in the joy of their reunion. Jasmine kicked up her back feet as she ran. More focused, Rosie reached Lucy first.

Lucy lured the cows back to their proper enclosure with the carrot tops. Hopefully, leaving the gate open had been a one-time mistake on Drake's part, because she couldn't very well lecture him about closing it when she didn't want him to know she'd come by in his absence.

After also doling out the apples, Lucy crossed the paddock to check the hay and water supply. Stocked, as usual. She both appreciated and resented that Drake took care of the cows. She wanted them to have good lives, but if Drake failed to see to their needs, she could involve the authorities to remove them from him and place them in her care, like they should've been for months now. After all, they were hers. Just not on paper.

Two weeks into her three-month relationship with Drake, she'd shown him a video of two mini Highland cows and had giggled about how cute they were. "I'd never get one, of course," she'd said.

Drake hadn't asked why, so she hadn't explained.

The next time he'd invited her out to his ranch, he'd introduced her to the newly acquired Rosie and Jasmine.

"You bought them for me?" she'd asked.

"Of course. What my girl wants, my girl gets."

"I said I'd never get one, though."

He shrugged. "I have the funds and the space."

"It wasn't that. I mean, those are obstacles too, but the breeding practices ..." She shrugged helplessly.

The cows were already there, so what good would it do to explain that Highland cattle didn't naturally come in mini size? Breeders got minis a few different ways. She didn't mind the idea of a Highland being crossed with a smaller breed, but some of the other practices included purposely breeding cattle with harmful gene mutations or separating calves from their mothers instead of giving them the chance to become big and strong on their mother's milk.

Drake waved off the concern without asking for details. "A petting zoo was offloading them because they're too big for some of the toddlers that come. They'd been looking for a buyer for months, and things weren't looking good for them. So you can rest easy. They're rescues."

"Oh. Well, in that case." A smile grew, and Lucy let herself into the pen.

Playful, affectionate, and easy to handle, the cows were everything she'd dreamed of. She'd never realized they would one day become leverage against her, keeping her in Drake's orbit long after the relationship had run its course.

Footsteps alerted her to Jasmine nosing a rubber kickball toward her. Lucy tossed it, and Jaz rolled it back again.

"You two behave more like dogs than my actual dog does." Lucy's lazy hound would chase a ball if she threw it, but then he'd stand next to it baying like he'd treed a coon instead of followed a ball to its resting place.

As the game of fetch continued, Rosie ambled up and stood beside her. Lucy petted her while launching the ball for Jaz. Scents of hay and manure mingled with juniper and pine and the mint-like coolness of a breeze winding through the mountain landscape. Snowy mountains hemmed in the pastures beneath a deep-blue Colorado sky.

Hard to believe Drake's place could be so peaceful. She should've snuck private visits sooner. Trouble was, her work hours overlapped with his. Even now, she needed to get to another appointment. Her limbs grew heavy at the thought of leaving so soon.

Finding the courage to sneak a visit wasn't enough. She prayed again that the Lord would cause Drake to get bored with her. To give her the cows to avoid their ongoing expense, his ongoing contact with her. Unfortunately, she suspected the only way he'd let Lucy go completely would be if he found someone new to control. She didn't want that for anyone. And even in that scenario, he might get rid of the cows some other way just to spite Lucy.

What would he do if he learned of this visit? Her bravado snapped like a rope under too heavy a load. Sneaking around like this probably wasn't what Second Timothy meant when it talked about power.

Whatever real power is, Lord, I need some of that so I can be free of Drake.

Another Bible verse rose like a counterpoint. *Truth will set you free.*

Well, that wasn't helpful—at least not in this situation, where the truth was, she wouldn't be free of Drake until she got her cows away from him. But just because that verse was the first thing to occur to her after she prayed didn't mean it was the Lord's final answer. She'd have to wait and see how He showed up in all of His power to right this situation.

She stood and dusted off. Rosie kept pace with her to the gate. Jasmine trotted ahead and stood blocking the way.

Lucy's heart sank. Was the cow purposely trying to keep her in? Or was she giving the animal too much credit? She scratched Jaz behind the ear. "Sorry, sweetie. I'll rescue you from here just as soon as I can."

Chapter Three

"Your wife must have recovered?" Lucy leaned against the doorframe that opened into the treatment room at Jack Carter's veterinary clinic.

He shut the supply cabinet and turned with a welcoming smile. "She's feeling much better. Thank you for your help this morning."

Lucy tucked her chin and leveled a knowing look at him. It'd been a long day. Thankfully, she hadn't heard a word from Drake about her secret visit with Rosie and Jasmine, but worry over it had drained her energy far more than her full day of appointments.

Jack stuffed his hands in the pockets of his lab coat, pulled them out again, and bustled to the sink to wash them nervously.

"What was wrong with her?" Lucy asked.

"Oh, a stomach bug." He stretched the words as if he was making them up as he went along.

"It's amazing she started so sick and recovered quickly enough to meet a friend at Donut Haven just as soon as I finished up at Price Quarter Horses."

"Oh. Well." Another pump of soap. "You know how stomach bugs can be. Intense one minute, better the next."

Lucy waited for him to stop with the handwashing. When he didn't, she said, "Clean hands won't help a dirty conscience."

Like a child slowly backing away from a cookie jar, Jack turned the lever on the faucet and the flow stopped. He took two towels from the dispenser and wiped his hands before turning toward her. He lowered his head and scratched behind his ear. Instead of a look of remorse, however, smile lines crinkled his face. "Go easy on me. It was Dolores's idea."

"Dolores told you to tell me she was sick this morning? Why ever would she do that?"

He sucked a breath through his teeth. "You see, Hollis has been going through a lot."

The muscles in Lucy's neck froze as fast as a road in an ice storm. She'd heard some rumors, of course. And, sure, her heart went out to the friendly cowboy with the thoughtful eyes, but what did his troubles have to do with Dolores's fake illness? "Okay ..."

"So have you."

Another seemingly unrelated fact. She narrowed her eyes. "How so?"

"That Drake guy ..." Jack shook his head. "That's what started it. Your parents told us about what that Drake guy was like, what he's doing to you."

Mom and Dad were so close with the Carters, Jack and Dolores were like an aunt and uncle to Lucy. It made sense they'd know some basics about what had occurred between her and Drake.

"Hollis had a run-in with him too, you know."

Lucy nodded. Thanks to the video, his falling out with Drake was common knowledge.

"Dolores had this idea that maybe ..."

"Maybe what?"

"I've known the Price boys as long as I've known you."

Since birth, then. But Hollis had spent the better part of the last eighteen-or-so years on the rodeo circuit and tending a ranch of his own in Texas, only visiting Redemption Ridge occasionally until his dad's health required someone to come take over Price Quarter Horses. Meanwhile, Lucy had left only for vet school and then returned to build a business of her own—a business Jack had been instrumental in helping to launch. Wherever this was going, the least she could do was let him tell the story.

"Hollis was a good boy. Sensible. Smart. Loyal, especially when it came to his family. I think that's why he kept on heading for Will right up until he retired, even though we all know he'd have won more often in team roping with a better heeler. It's also why, of the brothers, Hollis is the one who came back for his father."

General consensus around town was that Will should've been the one to sacrifice his rodeo career, since everyone thought he was riding Hollis's coattails. And maybe he had been. Will and his new team roping partner hadn't qualified for some of the bigger rodeos this year. But did a lack of rodeo skill make Will the best brother to care for an ailing father or take over the family business? Hardly.

If Hollis was the man Jack painted him to be, he was the one a father would want to step in. Still, it'd been quite a sacrifice. Hollis had earned a good deal of money competing, and by all accounts, he'd loved it. Training the next wave of champion roping horses might keep him in the industry, but surely the work was different.

"What I'm saying is, Hollis is a good man, like his father was." Jack stopped, as if he'd explained everything.

From the little she'd seen, she suspected he was right about Hollis. Hoped for it, really. In the aftermath of Drake, she needed to believe good guys were still out there. She liked the thought of Hollis, who'd ducked Chantal's advances, doted on his horse, and had sacrificed so much for his family, being one of them. Still, he was none of her business.

"Seems like you would've wanted to be there yourself this morning for a client when you have so much history with his whole family."

Jack wobbled his head. "How'd he seem to you?"

Lucy shrugged. "Fine. A little taken aback by Chantal, mostly concerned about his horse."

He raised a finger. "His *dad's* horse. Pepperjack's a Price horse, born and raised. Bill trained and rode him more years than Hollis did, and when the time came for Pep to retire from rodeo, Bill was more than happy to have him back. That horse is a rare one. A focused athlete when the time came, but always game for an easy trail ride and whatever snacks he can get." Jack chuckled. "Especially fond of stolen bagels, the rascal."

There was probably a story there, and he might prefer to tell it than to answer her initial question, but if she let him keep on like this, he'd never admit his true purpose in this morning's charade. "Enough, Jack. Just tell me. Why did you and Dolores conspire to send me out to treat Pepperjack?"

"It wasn't about Pep. It's about Hollis."

"Hollis." Saying his name prompted the memory of Pepperjack bumping his hat off—or trying to, anyway. Hollis had the lightning-fast reflexes that made him a star in timed rodeo events. She'd barely glimpsed his short, reddish-brown hair before he'd caught the hat and righted it again. But the part that had really stood out to her? The way amusement lit his eyes at the horse's antics. He had a soft spot for the horse, and a man who treated his animals well might show kindness in other relationships too.

The first warning sign she'd explained away about Drake? The way his animals were always on edge around him. Instead, she'd believed him when he claimed they were rescues he was rehabilitating.

She shook her head, clearing the thought. "What about Hollis?"

"He's sad. Getting by, sure, the way people do, but Dolores and I have found so much happiness and support in each other. I don't know what I would've done without her when my mother died."

Lucy's crossed arms suddenly loosened, and her hands bumped her thighs. "You were trying to set us up?"

"Well, you're lonely too, right? Piper and Graham have their little one now—not to mention her nephew's still living with them, right?"

Lucy nodded. She'd been nothing but happy for her best friend when she'd gotten married. If she'd realized how much more limited Piper's time would become, she might've been a little slower about encouraging her toward Graham.

Or not.

Graham and Piper were good together, and their baby was a huge blessing. Lucy couldn't resent that for them, even if it meant Jack was right: She was lonely. She hadn't realized it'd been that obvious.

Turned out, Jack wasn't finished taking inventory of her miseries. "Plus, things went sideways with you and that Drake guy."

"His name *is* Drake. No need to add 'that' and 'guy' every time."

He scrunched his nose so hard that his upper lip lifted. "How about the reverse? I'll call him 'that guy' and you'll know who I mean."

She glanced up at the perforated ceiling tiles. "How about

you don't worry about my dating life, and then none of this will matter."

He grunted. "I don't think Dolores will go for that."

"Jack. Come on. I'm in my thirties now. So is Hollis. We do not need matchmakers interfering in our lives." Even if the idea of them together ... No. She wasn't ready to go there.

"You could just date the man. Then I could get her to back off."

Just date the man? Her annoyance flared. She didn't like this much more than she liked Drake trying to push her around. "This isn't how it works, Jack. As far as I can tell, he's no more interested than I am."

"He said he wants a family."

A juicy bit of information, but context was everything, and something told her Jack was leaving a lot out. "Did he say he wanted you and Dolores to matchmake for him?"

Jack pressed his mouth into a line. "Sometimes, people need a little encouragement to move in the right direction. And since it's a direction he wants to go ..." He shrugged.

Her head started shaking all on its own, and as she became aware of the reflexive movement, she emphasized it. "No. If Drake taught me anything, it's that healthy boundaries are vital, so this is a boundary. I don't want to be set up with anyone right now. I won't be stepping in for any more calls to Price Quarter Horses."

Jack's shoulders slumped. "What's the harm?"

"What's the need for it?" Lucy countered. "You're concerned we're both sad or lonely, but it's Christmastime in Redemption Ridge. There are a gazillion events to attend with family and friends, not to mention daily reminders that Jesus came to give us what we most need. And that's not a date."

He sighed heavily. "Okay. I'll tell Dolores I tried."

Finally. She'd stood her ground. Had come out ahead. "Also tell her to *stop* trying, okay?"

"I'll pass along the message, but she's got her heart set on a Christmas romance."

"Then tell her to go buy one from Bethany's Book Barn." She left, chin up and shoulders back. Jack and Dolores meant well, but only time would tell if they were any better at honoring boundaries than Drake was.

Chapter Four

With twinkle lights, evergreen garland, red velvet bows, and white linens, Redemption Ridge Ranch had once again set a magical scene for the annual barn dance. The inaugural event of the Christmas season brought together the who's-who of the community, and Lucy greeted at least ten friends, church acquaintances, and customers before she spotted Piper's table.

On seeing her, Piper's mouth formed an O. When Lucy got close enough to hear over the music, Piper said, "That looks even prettier in person—and it looked pretty in pictures."

Lucy laid her coat on a chair back and smoothed her hands over the cobalt-blue dress. Usually, she and Piper shopped for this event together, but not this time. Piper hadn't been getting out much in the three months since welcoming her firstborn, Jasper. Piper lifted a hand from patting her baby's back to motion Lucy to turn a circle.

She would've been more willing if it were just her and her best friend at the table, but Piper's husband, Graham, sat with his arm around his wife's shoulders. Next to him, his best friend, Cody, nodded hello. Piper's nephew, Bryce, who lived with Piper and Graham, sat by them too, but he and a friend focused on a phone. Beyond them, the size of the crowd had to be part of the reason it was so warm in the room.

Hoping most people were wrapped up in their own interactions, Lucy turned a demure circle with just enough flair that her dress fluttered around her knees.

"Lovely!" Piper shifted Jasper from one arm to the other.

The baby lifted a pudgy hand toward Graham and cooed.

"Is it my turn?" Graham held his hands toward his son, and Jasper's head wobbled with excitement.

Piper passed him over and stood. Her black velvet dress looked soft in the glowing light. "Mind if we go get punch?"

"We're fine here." Graham's attention shifted to Lucy. "But Piper hasn't worn heels in a year."

Lucy snorted as Piper scoffed. Though Piper was not *always* to blame for the things that happened to her, the woman was more accident-prone than most. With an infant to care for, she couldn't afford to twist or break anything tonight. Lucy gave a laughing nod to Graham and threaded her arm through Piper's.

Piper sighed a dramatic complaint, but she also squeezed Lucy's arm. "Let's see about some of Connie's famous Cowboy Christmas Cider. I also haven't tried *that* in a year."

Apparently, others felt equally deprived, because they ended up standing in a line three people deep. Given how intent everyone was on chatting, they'd be here a few minutes.

"I think Jasper has started rolling over—but he's very covert about it." Piper's beaming face pointed toward the dance floor, where people moved to a lively beat, but Lucy doubted she saw the dancers. Instead, she was probably trying to glimpse her husband and child, who sat on the other side of the room.

"A couple of times now, I put him on his back, but when I

came in again a few minutes later, I found him on his tummy. So, Graham and I decided a stakeout was in order. I put him down and we waited around the corner in the hallway, but then we got, um, distracted, and next thing we knew, he was on his tummy."

"Distracted?" Lucy asked dryly.

Piper shrugged. "What can I say? Fatherhood looks good on him, and I've always enjoyed kissing the man."

Lucy lifted a hand. "And that's all the detail I need."

Piper jostled their interlinked arms. "When are you going to find someone you enjoy kissing?"

Considering Lucy had encouraged her toward Graham, she couldn't complain too much about her friend taking an interest in her love life. Still, she missed the way Piper hadn't pressured her back during the days when Piper had sworn off relationships herself. "You know a good relationship isn't based on physical attraction."

"True, but it doesn't hurt."

Lucy chose silence, because the physical aspect of a relationship *could* hurt. Kissing Drake had been fun at first, and she'd taken that as yet another sign that she'd finally found a good match. But the more his nice guy act wore off, the more his true personality showed through in every aspect of their relationship. His kisses became sloppy at best, demanding at worst. What they'd shared early on had simply been another layer of hurt to sort through when it'd all fallen apart.

A broad and tall man in a navy-blue suit bumped between couples as he cut across the corner of the dance floor. His modern pompadour hairstyle was as slick as the smile of apology he offered to the dancers he'd interrupted. Did they consider he could've avoided the intrusions if he'd simply gone a couple of feet out of his way to skirt the dance floor instead of traipsing across it?

"Speaking of ..."

"Huh?" Piper followed Lucy's glare. "Oh. Drake." Her mouth puckered with distaste.

Anxiety fluttered like a flock of pigeons determined to roost in her chest. He might not be headed her way. He lived and had an office a town over, but business and networking frequently brought him to Redemption Ridge. After all, Redemption Ridge's local lawyer Ruby Thompson was diligent and sharp, but even she couldn't represent both sides of a dispute. Hopefully, Drake had more important people to schmooze and would leave Lucy alone.

But what if he knew about her visit? He might be looking for her. Could she stand her ground?

The truth will set you free. But what truth? That she'd ventured onto his property without permission? That she couldn't stand his company? She couldn't see either of those conversations going well.

Finally, the people ahead of them moved off.

Lucy motioned Piper ahead toward the punch table. "Let's get our drinks and get back to the table. He won't bother me there." Not when their friend group included more than a couple of police officers and loyal friends who'd see through his false niceties and backhanded compliments. Drake prized his reputation too much to make a public scene.

"Okay." Piper claimed the punch ladle and a cup.

Lucy fidgeted and glanced over. Drake's eyes had locked on her.

"Oh no!" Piper's exclamation brought Lucy's attention back to where a spill raced across the tabletop. Piper dove on the stack of napkins and blotted like their lives depended on it. "I'm so sorry. I can't believe I did that."

"It's okay." Lucy joined her in mopping up.

Maybe, if they kept their heads down, Drake would keep moving.

"Not much has changed, I see." His voice came smooth and low from the opposite side of the table.

Lucy swallowed hard, bracing herself mentally before straightening. "Drake. How are you?"

"I'm well." Despite the line that had formed behind Lucy and Piper, he helped himself to the ladle and poured a cup of punch. "You'd know that if you'd arranged your last visit to my ranch when I was home, instead of trespassing."

Panic lanced her stomach. He must've had a camera she didn't know about. Or a nosy neighbor.

Eyes wide, Piper shoved the sopping wet napkins in the now-empty cup and poured herself a new one.

"I was treating clients in your area. It only made sense to visit with Rosie and Jasmine while I was close by, instead of making the extra trip." She smiled like she had no doubt about how understanding he'd be. "Saved me almost an hour of driving time."

"Your access to my property is a favor. If you would prefer to avoid me, you're not required to come at all."

Lucy gulped. Jasmine and Rosie adored attention, and Drake didn't give them any. "You bought them for me."

"The heifers? I acquired them during our relationship, but the cattle are in my name, on my property, and I'm liable for what happens on my land. That means I can't have visitors wandering around unattended."

"She's a vet." Piper's voice was incredulous. "She can handle herself around animals."

Incredulity skewed Drake's eyebrows, his focus entirely on Lucy. "The way you roll around with those cows, you could easily be injured. I can't have you lying in a pasture, waiting hours for help, on my property."

She didn't "roll around" with them, but letting them near her face had been too much for Drake from early on. Within a week of him buying the cattle, he labeled her relationship with them "undignified."

Shame chipped away at her spine, but she willed herself not to crumble. Not to be bossed around or belittled. "I'm still happy to move them somewhere else. That way, you wouldn't have to feel so responsible."

"Responsibility isn't a feeling." He spoke with the finality of a judge pronouncing a prison sentence. "I'll be keeping my cattle, and if you'd like to remain welcome to visit them, you'll come when I'm available to accompany you."

Panic became real and hard in the center of Lucy's chest. What could she do but agree? "Understood."

Piper bit her lip, forehead furrowed. But even her friend, who could be feisty when she wanted to be, didn't speak up. How could she? How could anyone? Drake owned two animals Lucy loved like her own pets. And because of it, he had power over her.

"Good. With that out of the way ..." His handsome face pulled into a smile she knew better than to trust. "Here alone?"

"No." To prove the point, she poured two cups of punch. If no one at her table wanted one, she'd drink both herself.

"Come on, Lucy. I know the truth." His eyebrows twitched upward. "You never should've ended things between us."

"We'll have to agree to disagree." She nodded for Piper, who stood between Lucy and their table, to head back.

Piper obliged, but Drake cut into Lucy's path, so close she could smell the sweet aroma of his cologne. To think she'd once enjoyed that scent. Piper's eyes darted, taking in the scene, then she hurried off. To get reinforcements perhaps?

Shame returned, torching her cheeks this time. She should be able to handle Drake better than this.

"When are you going to realize I'm the best thing that

could've happened to you?" His tone was cajoling. "I've been patient, waiting for you to sort through your issues, but don't you think it's time to come back?"

She didn't know what to do about her cows, but this, at least, she had an answer for. "I didn't ask for a break. I ended things. And I never should've apologized when I did it. You lied to and manipulated me until I didn't know which end was up. My only mistake was trusting you to begin with."

Drake's eyes widened with surprise that made her confidence wobble. "Lied to you? When?"

"Take your pick." For one thing, he'd said Rosie and Jasmine were hers. But they'd already been over that tonight, and Lucy had no new cards to play. "How about when you said you wanted me to help at the Turner ranch because they were longtime friends of yours who couldn't afford another vet bill right then?"

"That wasn't a lie."

"They're your clients, not your friends, and they were considering finding new representation. You offered my services to their ranch as a perk to keep them as customers."

"I saw a need and knew you'd want to help."

"And how did *you* help? Did you do some pro bono work for them? Or did you keep right on charging four hundred dollars an hour?"

"I do not charge that much."

Maybe it was more like three hundred. Her point stood, but an inaccuracy in a conversation with Drake meant giving him the upper hand. Where he was concerned, mistakes like that cost people their life savings and self-respect.

Lucy's hands shook, still holding two cups of punch that her sour stomach wouldn't allow her to drink. "It's over, Drake."

"Don't be like this, Luce. You're alone tonight, right? I

understand you, and this business about Rosie and Jasmine needn't be so uncomfortable. Don't exaggerate—"

"There you are." An arm encircled her shoulders. Meanwhile, one of the cups of punch was lifted from her grasp by a masculine hand with a surprisingly gentle touch. Stunned, her line of sight followed the cup to a set of lips as the man took a drink.

Hollis stood beside her, the shadow of stubble on his jaw at her eye level. He wore a crisp black hat and shirt. When he lowered the cup, it was half-empty. He nodded to the other glass. "Drink up. They haven't been playing many slow songs, so let's not miss this one."

Hollis was pretending to be her date?

Lucy blinked. Was this the right path? She lifted her foot to step away, then thought better of it. Hollis was the fastest way out of this conversation with Drake. "We can leave our drinks at the table."

Hollis lowered his arm from around her and threaded their fingers together. "Lead the way, Doc."

Doc? Did that sound like a term of endearment befitting a romance? If she paused to question it, Drake would see through their already shaky performance. She flashed her ex a quick smile that might have looked a little more like a sneer than she'd intended and hurried away.

* * *

Hollis followed Dr. Lucy away from Drake, half expecting a hand on his shoulder to pull him back for a confrontation. It never came. The element of surprise might've saved them, and by the look on his friend Clint Taylor's face, Drake wasn't the only one who noticed Hollis threading through the crowd with the doctor's hand in his. Thankfully, Clint was a little too smitten with his new wife, Nora, to leave her on the dance floor and tease out an explanation.

Hollis recognized most of the people at the table Lucy led him to. Cody Adams and Graham Lockhart served on the police force. Graham's wife, Piper, had grown up in Redemption Ridge and owned a business downtown.

The tension in Piper's shoulders relaxed when she spotted Lucy. "Oh, good. You got away."

Then her line of sight fell to Lucy and Hollis's linked hands and her eyes bugged wide.

Lucy's fingers straightened, but he didn't let her pull away. "He's probably watching. Better follow through." The first strains of the song had been playing when he'd suggested they dance. Now, Chris Young's voice streamed over the speakers.

"Oh." Her hand stilled in his, except for a tremble.

Hollis had known Drake was a snake. He hadn't realized how nasty of one he could be until he'd been in line for punch, just close enough to overhear Drake steamrolling the compassionate and intelligent Dr. Lucy Aveline.

Though he didn't seek out gossip, Hollis had heard over the summer that the two were dating, and then fall brought news of their split. Since it'd taken Hollis a while to see Drake's true colors, he couldn't blame Lucy for not realizing sooner what she'd gotten into with the man. Based on what he'd just witnessed, she'd been the one to end it.

She'd said the right things to Drake, but the tremor in her voice as she'd done so had pushed Hollis into action. And now he was ... doing what, exactly? Faking a relationship?

Well, it was only for one night. Maybe only for a song or two, if Drake would leave. And Hollis didn't hate the idea of spending time with Dr. Lucy. The opposite, actually.

As he'd suspected, she looked even more like a princess when she wasn't outfitted for work. Tonight, her dress was so blue it practically glowed over the soft curves of her slim figure.

Hollis led her into the thick of the crowd on the dance floor so other partygoers would act as a screen between them and Drake. Clint danced with Nora about fifteen feet away. He lifted a hand in question and mouthed something toward Hollis over Nora's shoulder.

Hollis wasn't that good at reading lips, but he could guess what Clint wanted. He mouthed the word "Later" back.

Clint frowned. Nora followed her husband's gaze, spotted Hollis, and waved hello.

He nodded back and refocused on Lucy. They were as deep into the crowd as they were going to get. He turned toward her and lifted his hands in an offer to dance.

Lucy's hand settled on his shoulder, light as a sparrow. "Fitting that our first dance is to a song called 'Rescue Me,' I guess." Her eyebrows drew low as she glanced around.

If she kept looking that nervous, one more glimpse of them would reveal the truth to Drake.

"I don't see you as someone in need of rescue." Hollis rested one hand on her waist and captured her other hand in his.

Her attention zipped back to him. Could she read his expression, his determination to shield her? Whatever she saw, she looked away again and asked, "So why'd you swoop in?"

"From the sounds of it, we have a common ..." Enemy sounded like too strong of a word. "Adversary. Giving you an easy escape from one difficult conversation doesn't mean you can't fend for yourself."

As they danced, a fragrance floated on the air around her, as fresh as newly cut grass and layered like the scent of a florist shop. She moved easily with him, her side warm beneath his hand.

This was not a chore at all.

"Besides," he said, "most of this song is about the man needing rescue."

One eyebrow quirked. "The man, huh?"

He laughed at her teasing, but it rang hollow. He was well aware of how much he needed saving. He'd gone all in on family, certain he was doing the right thing, and yet somehow, he'd never felt more alone or lost. If Hollis couldn't turn things around at the ranch, they'd lose it. Which, of course, was too much to throw on Dr. Lucy. "Don't we all need rescue? I imagine that's why I've been seeing you at church every week."

"True. But even Drake's a regular attender at church—he goes to one closer to his house instead of driving into Redemption Ridge." The corner of her mouth bit into her cheek, as if there was more she wanted to say.

"I can't speak for him, but I go to church because I can't save myself, and I'm grateful that, because of Jesus, I don't have to." He felt like a bit of a fraud saying that. His belief ought to temper how he felt about his dad, ought to give him hope about the business. Did the heaviness that cloaked him point to a problem with his faith?

Dr. Lucy nodded. "Amen."

The song wound down, and regret slowed Hollis's movements. He shouldn't have wasted this dance by thinking about his own problems.

She snuggled up to his shoulder, and every thought slipped away, replaced by warmth and contentedness. "Drake's still here," she murmured. "I think he's keeping an eye on us."

Ah, so it wasn't that she wanted to draw close.

He steeled himself against the disappointment. What had he really expected? That Lucy was walking around with her heart on her sleeve the way he seemed to be doing? "I'm happy to stick together. We can even come back to dancing, but I do owe cider to some of the people back at my table. The whole reason I overheard Drake was because they sent me for drinks."

She chuckled as the song ended and she stepped back. "How did you end up being their server?"

"I only came tonight because my mom insisted on having my company. Of course, as soon as we got here, she found friends. The punch is for her and the Carters."

Lucy's eyebrows lifted. "The Carters?"

"Yeah. They're longtime friends of my parents. Yours, too, I gathered. They're all together." He hiked his thumb toward the table where he'd left them, though he hadn't looked their way once since he'd interrupted Lucy and Drake's conversation.

Lucy's mouth pressed into a line. If her nearness had been an unexpected ray of sunshine, her expression now was the clouds rolling back in.

"Everything okay?" he asked.

"Peachy." She motioned, and they returned to the punch table.

There, he managed to corral three cups. Lucy carried two more for her own parents, quiet as she followed him to the table.

Her dad stood to greet her, and she passed him a cup of punch before patting his back in a half-hug. She set the other cup before her mother and kissed her cheek. Whatever her frustration, it wasn't with her folks.

Hollis lowered the trio of drinks he carried to the table between Dolores Carter and his mom, then rubbed his mom's shoulder. "Dr. Lucy, have you met my mom, Susan Price?"

"Not officially." Lucy extended her hand. "Hi, Mrs. Price."

"Call me Susan." Mom gave her hand a squeeze.

"Speaking of"— Dolores's twinkling eyes peered toward Lucy—"isn't *Doctor* Lucy a little formal, dear?"

It'd sounded that way to his own ears. Since he'd taken her hand, he'd felt a connection with her that went beyond veterinarian/client, and he'd started to drop the title in his mind.

But Lucy's chin dipped in a sort of "game on" posture Hollis wasn't quite sure what to make of. "It is what my clients call me."

Good thing he'd kept the formality any time he'd spoken aloud, then.

"Psh." Dolores swiped her hand through the air. "You just shared such a lovely dance. Surely, you're on a first-name basis."

The corners of Dr. Lucy's mouth tightened.

"She worked long and hard for the degree," he said. "I have no problem calling her by the title she earned." Especially if it meant not stepping in the middle of whatever drama was unfolding here.

That earned him a nod of appreciation, and then her keen gaze tracked something beyond him. "Thanks for your help, Hollis, but it looks like we're free to go our own ways."

He turned as Drake disappeared through the exit. By the time he brought his attention back, Lucy—*Dr.* Lucy—was already retreating.

And Clint was advancing. He tipped his head for Hollis to step away from the table with him. Clint was a more faithful friend than Hollis's own brother had been in recent years. He had a right to ask about Dr. Lucy, so Hollis obliged.

"Drake's ex?" Clint asked. "You sure she's not a spy or something?"

Hollis laughed, but he understood the sentiment. "I think he pulled one over on her just like he did me. Actually, it was probably worse for her."

Clint crossed his arms. "Nora said she's good people too. I guess Lucy introduced herself once to ask after Ovation, but

Ovation's why I'm concerned. I hate what he did to you, to the horse. If he's pulling the strings here—"

"Dr. Lucy and I have mutual friends." And from back at the table, Dolores and Jack watched him with interest. Earlier in the night, they'd been singing Lucy's praises and hinting at how deeply Drake had hurt her. "She's a victim of his, not an ally. I trust her."

"Okay. If you're sure." Clint's mouth settled in a grim line. "Just don't let him up his tally."

"His tally?"

"Of victims."

Hollis took his hat off just long enough to run a hand over his hair. Settling it once again, he said, "I'm not doing business with him anymore. Hopefully, we're beyond that."

"Hopefully, but would you really put it past him to find a way to be a problem?"

Given how the man had hurt Dr. Lucy? No, he really wouldn't.

Chapter Five

Based on the speed of their departure from church the following morning, Lucy suspected Jack and Dolores knew she'd be looking for them. Lucy zipped her coat and jogged from the building. The thirty-something-degree air breezed through the material of her dress pants, chilling her legs, but this conversation shouldn't take long.

"Jack! Dolores!" She waved after the older couple as she passed the first row of cars.

They turned in tandem, Jack's arm around his wife's shoulders. Short, plump, and eternally cheerful, Dolores could serve as Mrs. Claus, especially when her cheeks were pink from the cool weather, as they were now. Jack didn't much resemble Santa, except that his eyes held a slight twinkle as Lucy drew to a stop.

She tied the belt on her wool coat tighter against the cold. "That was no coincidence last night, was it?"

"What, dear?" Dolores looked the picture of innocence and curiosity.

Lucy shook her head. "I already told Jack. I have no desire

to be the subject of a matchmaking plot. Please don't make this more awkward than it already is."

"Oh, it's not awkward." Dolores tweaked her elbow. "We know a good match when we see one, don't we, honey?"

Jack shrugged. The twinkle deepened.

In some respects, spending time with Hollis had felt like a good fit. The man had a true soft spot for his horse, swept her away from her toxic ex, openly admitted his need for Jesus, and held her on the dance floor with respect and care. But even counting the time in the barn, treating Pepperjack, they'd spent less than an hour together. A man could fake anything for sixty minutes. He could fake kindness for a month or two.

She shook her hands. "You know about Drake."

"And how Hollis saved you from him last night?" Dolores asked. "Very heroic. We all thought so."

We all? Lucy's eyes sank closed. "Are our parents in on this?"

"On what, dear?" Dolores blinked and clasped her hands over her chest.

Jack sighed. "No use denying it, Lola. She already knows you weren't sick, and you just used the word 'match' yourself."

Dolores chuckled lightly. "In that case, no, your parents aren't involved. Not in so many words. But Susan would love to see her son happy, and he himself said he'd like a family. 'Family's everything.' That's a direct quote. He's gonna need love if he wants one for himself."

Lucy exhaled a white breath. "But *I'm* not looking for a new relationship. I explained this to Jack. I need you to respect that."

"We only asked for some punch." Dolores laughed.

"*After* you watched me get in line?"

"Seemed like as good a time as any. And that dance." Her shoulders shook with what Lucy might have credited to a shiver if not for the delight on her face. "You two have chemistry."

"The dance was about avoiding Drake." Even if she had been fighting the urge to trail her fingers along the collar of Hollis's shirt and up into his hair. Attraction was as useless as first impressions for judging a relationship's potential, because at one point, she'd felt a similar draw toward Drake. "Is that really what you want for Hollis? Someone who's using him to avoid someone else?"

When she put it that way, she might owe him an apology, in fact.

Dolores scrunched her nose. "Relationships have started in worse ways. You just need someone to help you believe in love again. And he needs someone to cheer him up. Keep him company. Help him get out more. When he first came back, he devoted himself to his parents and the business out of necessity. But now Bill's been gone the better part of a year, and he's still doing nothing but moping and working. It's enough to break a mother's heart."

"He isn't your son."

"But I'm close with Susan." Her expression turned downright mournful. "Need I remind you it's her first Christmas without Bill? And you should take that to heart, because if true love doesn't exist, then why's she so sad?"

Lucy opened her mouth but choked on any reply she might've offered. Her nose stung, and it wasn't the cold. "It's not that I don't believe in love."

Dolores continued as if she hadn't spoken. "She asked us to help keep her mind off things, so we've packed our calendar with events to attend together, and just last night, your parents signed on for the fun too. I'm sure they'd love to have you join us. The more the merrier! Hollis is such a good son, he agreed to accompany Susan whenever she asks."

This was worse than she'd thought. The more time the

Carters spent with Hollis, the more likely they'd encourage him in her direction like they encouraged her in his. What would those speeches sound like? Probably gossip-laced tales of how awful Drake had been to her.

And he had been. Why had it taken her months to see it? Because he hadn't crushed her. She would've noticed that. He'd shrunk her down with snide comment after outright lie, until one day she realized anytime she was around him, she felt small and helpless. She refused to feel that way a second longer than she had to.

Because of Rosie and Jasmine, Drake could still push her around some, but she would not add to that list by letting the Carters—well-intentioned or not—force her into anything.

"Look." She rubbed her quickly-cooling hands. "Dating isn't the only cure for sad loneliness. If you're worried about Hollis, what he needs is friends, and I'm happy to invite him to join me and my friends for all the big Christmas events. As a friend."

Dolores bit her lip and looked from Jack to Lucy. "If you're so very sure you don't want to date, maybe you know some nice single ladies?"

She laughed and rubbed her forehead. "Some, but—"

"Wonderful!" Dolores clapped. "With you on the case, I'm sure he'll find someone in no time."

Lucy inched backward. "I'm not a matchmaker, Dolores. What I meant—"

"The way I see it, you have two choices." The older woman's jovial features took on an oddly cool glint. "One, let us make arrangements, or, two, you can do the honors. That's the only way we'll step back and let you take the reins."

"If paths cross, I will make introductions, but—"

"See that you do, dear. We'll be ready to step in if things aren't going well."

"Dolores ..." Lucy looked to Jack for help, but the man

just smiled down at his wife like she was the most entertainment he'd had all year.

Dolores reached up as if to pat her cheek, but her height forced her to settle for Lucy's shoulder instead. "Remember, we're spending the whole month with both of your parents. We can be *a lot* more hassle than we've been thus far."

Lucy wouldn't be so worried if Dolores was wrong about the chemistry with Hollis. As it was, if she was pushed toward him too many times, she just might imagine herself in love—and wind up in another regrettable relationship. The last thing she needed was to be the target of a matchmaking scheme.

If avoiding a mess like that meant pointing the attention on someone else, so be it.

* * *

On Monday morning, yellow sun slanted into the Price Quarter Horses barn from the east and danced on dust motes and honey-colored walls. Such peaceful mornings reminded Hollis of his childhood when the horse barn had just a handful of stalls with no indoor arena. In those days, Pepperjack had been an energetic dark-gray foal, a product of the Price Quarter Horses herd. Hollis helped Dad train Pep one skill at a time until, when Pep was six and Hollis twelve, they began specialized training for tie-down roping. It wasn't long before Pepperjack was Dad's most trusted mount in rodeos.

Preparing for a trail ride, Hollis smoothed the saddle pad over Pep's now mostly-white coat and stepped back into the tack room for the saddle.

Hard-hitting footsteps advanced up the breezeway, too steady and fast to belong to Frank. Also, Frank would never venture into the barn without his hat, but the figure Hollis spotted as he left the tack room had nothing but slicked-back hair on his head.

"Who's Lucy Aveline to you?" Drake pushed back his suit jacket to put his fists on his hips.

Denying him his full attention, Hollis lifted the saddle onto Pep's back. "You're not a client here, so I'd thank you to leave."

"I know it can't be serious," Drake said.

Hollis circled the horse to let down the cinch, then came back around to tie it. He didn't want to lie. Hadn't yet. Well, perhaps in action by acting like Dr. Lucy was his date at the barn dance, but not in word. As he'd said, they hadn't played many slow songs that night, and once the idea to dance with her had occurred to him, he hadn't wanted to miss it.

He didn't figure he owed Drake an explanation, so he chose not to comment. With any luck, Drake would interpret his silence as confirmation of a relationship.

Why did he want that?

To bother Drake, mostly. But the guy might leave Lucy alone if Drake thought she was spoken for. Besides, Lucy had a lot going for her. A guy could do worse. A lot worse.

"I'm surprised you even have time to see somebody right now, what with your business troubles."

His back toward Drake, he clenched his teeth. Dad had been both a dreamer and generous to a fault. He'd mortgaged the ranch to help fund Will's ill-fated venture into real estate. Dad would've drained his retirement savings too if Hollis hadn't stepped up with a sizeable investment himself to provide the rest of what Will needed. The deal fell through in the worst possible way, as Hollis had suspected it would. Hollis lost a huge chunk of his savings, while Dad was stuck with a thirty-year mortgage on land that had been in the family for generations.

Will's promise to help with payments proved empty. Somehow, though they'd been raised by the same parents, the brothers didn't share the same commitment to coming through for family.

Then Dad got passionate about turning Price Quarter Horses into the premier roping horse training center in the nation, but no bank would lend him more.

Undeterred, Dad took money from private investors at high interest rates. The idea had been that once he had the new stable, indoor and outdoor arenas, and turnout areas, he'd attract top-paying clients. With that income stream, he planned to qualify for a traditional loan that would pay off the private investors before those debts came due. He'd then make the payments to the bank until the ranch was theirs again, free and clear.

The financial gymnastics might've worked, if Dad hadn't been diagnosed with bone cancer before the paint had dried on the new fences.

Dad's inability to work combined with medical bills to multiply his parents' debt. Hollis had again used his savings to pay off the medical expenses. What he didn't have was the lump sum to pay back Dad's private investors, whose loans were coming due next summer.

They needed the ranch to earn an income.

Unfortunately, as a new trainer, he couldn't charge as much as his dad had. Especially not after Drake publicly blamed him for traumatizing Ovation.

Hollis reviewed Pepperjack to ensure their visitor hadn't distracted him from any necessary step. The last thing he needed was to give Drake a story about a legitimate oversight.

Everything looked good.

He'd planned to go out the back, but he led Pepperjack toward the front. "I'll walk you out."

Drake fell into step beside him. "You sure she's worth it?"

Hollis spared him a glance.

Drake shrugged carelessly. "Wouldn't want to see you lose more business than you already have."

"Are you threatening me?"

"Only if you see me protecting Lucy as a threat. She's too trusting for her own good. I was going to leave well enough alone, but to show Lucy the truth about the man she's involved with? Well, that's worth a lot of time and energy."

Fury fired through Hollis's veins. Violently twisting the truth wouldn't wrench it from Hollis's grasp. He hadn't been raised to give up when the stakes were high. And the stakes didn't get much higher than shielding an innocent from a wolf like Drake.

Jaw clamped tight to keep unhelpful comments to himself, Hollis led Pepperjack into the drive.

Drake followed. "I have a good reputation, and I talk to a lot of people."

"Me too." Hollis tightened the saddle, then mounted. If Drake wanted to keep threatening him, he'd have to do it looking up from a couple of feet below.

Drake crossed his arms and surveyed the property. "How many generations has this place been in your family?"

Another threat? Drake clearly wanted to rattle him, and the best response would be to show him he'd failed.

If he gave Drake another glance, the man would undoubtedly see the anger burning in Hollis's eyes, so he dipped his chin and steered Pep away. "You have a nice afternoon."

"You too, Price."

Hollis prepared to stay near the house if Drake dawdled, but a moment later, his truck roared down the drive and off the property.

Chapter Six

Why hadn't she considered sooner how awkward it would be to invite Hollis to holiday events with her friends? Lucy stared through the windshield, on alert in case a deer or elk decided to cross the road in front of her truck on her way out to Price Quarter Horses. Freezing wind buffeted her vehicle, but thankfully the roads were clear and the sun shone.

She'd put this errand off, but with the next Christmas event—and the Carters' threats—looming, she had to act. So, she turned onto the drive that led to the stable. Her misgivings bucked like a prize bronc. How would she explain the random invitation to an entire roster of events? Why would he say yes?

Hollis was famous—at least in certain circles. He must have more friends than Jack and Dolores knew. Unless the Carters did know his friends and didn't count them because of their crazy idea that Hollis belonged with her.

But then there was their claim that Hollis was sad. A couple of times, as she'd treated Pepperjack, she'd looked up from her work to find his mouth curved in a mindless frown, a line set between his brows. When he didn't realize anyone was paying attention, sadness really did creep into his expression. She'd seen it at the barn dance too.

Dolores and Jack focused on how he'd lost his father. And that was bad enough, but he'd lost even more. He'd walked away from his old way of life and a job he'd loved to move back to his hometown.

Maybe Hollis could use a friend. Or at least a string of distractions to get him through Christmas like the Carters had offered Susan. Maybe he'd be happy to accept her invitation.

It wasn't as if she could turn back now anyway. Pastures with only the occasional scrubby tree surrounded the drive. Someone had likely spotted her coming, either from the house off to the right or the stable ahead. Turning around would raise more questions than they'd likely already have for her.

She parked by the stable and got out.

Even the near-freezing air held the scents of hay and horses.

Inside the stable, Lucy approached a wheelbarrow and the scraping sound that suggested someone was mucking stalls. Hopefully, Hollis himself so she could get her errand over with.

She stopped at the door of the stall and found herself face-to-face with Susan, who held a loaded manure rake. "Dr. Lucy. Nice to see you again."

She nearly withered in humiliation on the spot. This was awkward enough without having to navigate a conversation with Hollis's mom. Who knew what the Carters had told the woman. Lucy backed out of the way. "It's good to see you too, Mrs. Price."

"Susan." She dumped the contents of her shovel into the wheelbarrow and turned back with a smile. "Especially if you're going to be spending time out here."

Her wording suggested she knew the visit wasn't about business. She might credit Lucy's visit to anything from a new friendship to a twisty matchmaking plot, but Lucy couldn't think of a tactful way to ask what Susan had concluded. "Is Hollis around?"

Why did she have to sound like a nervous teenager?

Probably because her whole mission was approximately as mature as something a schoolgirl would dream up. To think sixty-something Dolores was behind it all.

"Sure." Susan pointed with her head, since the rake occupied her hands. "He's in the office. Right across from Pepperjack's stall."

"Okay. Thank you." Lucy headed away and knew she was getting close when the scent of coffee met her. She peeked in at Pepperjack, petted the horse's nose, then stepped into the office.

No one sat at the cluttered wooden desk. Cabinets and crowded bulletin boards covered the walls. Hollis stood in the corner, pouring himself a cup of coffee. He replaced the pot and rubbed his face before weighted steps brought him toward the desk.

The brim of his hat—the worn, brown one—angled toward her. He halted and brought his chin up until the brim allowed his thoughtful blue-gray eyes to fix on her. His lips lifted with gentle kindness that struck her as authentic, not showy the way Drake so often was. "Dr. Lucy. To what do I owe the pleasure?"

"We're being set up." Her spontaneous words ripped off the bandage, and her face stung accordingly.

He remained still, mouth still curved in a small smile, gaze on her. "Set up?"

"By Jack and Dolores. She wasn't sick the day Jack sent me here, and they didn't suddenly get thirsty at the dance. They saw me in line."

"Oh." He squinted, restarted for his desk, stopped again, and pointed at the coffeemaker. "You want some? It's fresh."

"You're not surprised?" It might've been rude to ignore his question, but her brain refused to get off the track it'd jumped on.

"I didn't ask for it, but surprised? No." Hollis took his seat. The office was heated, but he wore his canvas jacket open over a blue flannel as though he'd only stopped by the office briefly. His hands on his coffee cup looked strong and a little dusty, as fitting for a man who worked hard to earn an honest living. "But they've been asking a few too many questions about my dating life and aspirations of having a family for me to be surprised."

He spoke casually, as if he hadn't minded the inquisition, and suddenly, she wanted to know not only the questions they'd asked, but also his answers.

Did he have a dating life?

How interested in a family was he?

He sipped his coffee and motioned to the chair across from his desk. "You're surprised?"

She lowered herself onto the seat and tried to curb her curiosity. "I've been very clear I'm not interested in dating right now."

"Oh." He frowned and nodded once. "Like I said, it wasn't my idea. I didn't know what they were doing."

"But you don't mind." Her debate about what to say left her throat aching with conflicting orders to stop her words or let them rise. Perhaps it sounded like she was fishing for him to say he didn't mind being set up with her specifically. That wasn't how she'd wanted it to sound. She tried again. "You don't mind other people setting you up?"

"I've got bigger problems. It seems one of them is a problem for you too."

"Drake." Each word of the conversation she'd endured with her ex at the dance piled onto her shoulders.

His lips thinned in confirmation. "I'm sorry if I was out of line, acting like we were together. I know how he can be, and I wanted to make him back off. You deserve better than the way he was treating you."

Lucy crossed her ankles and pushed them against each other, trying hard not to fidget. "You two had a run-in too. Over Ovation?"

"He said Ovation's problems came from his last trainer." Hollis sighed and stared blankly toward the hall. "I know now there was no other trainer, but at the time I figured Drake hired someone else before me. Since my friend Clint married Nora St. Clair, whose family sold Ovation to Drake, I knew the horse had a solid start. Nora was pretty sad to learn what had become of him after he left their ranch. With Ovation's change in behavior being pretty recent, I thought it might not be irreversible.

"Clint rehabs horses, so he helped me figure out how to get Ovation past his hangups. We had him in great shape before he left my training program—beyond his issues *and* a solid roping horse to boot. But one week back home with Drake undid all of the progress we made. He's to blame and no one else, but he posted a video that claims I'm responsible."

"I saw."

Hollis tapped the desk. "For Ovation's sake, I tried to work out a solution, but I also couldn't leave myself open to more attacks. We couldn't come to an agreement." Hollis adjusted his coat. "Couldn't help overhearing last night that he's lied to you."

"Constantly. For one, he said he'd rescued Ovation from a rough situation and hired you to rehab him like he was some kind of benevolent hero. But toward the end of our relationship, when I was beginning to suspect Drake's real personality, I met Nora. Like you said, Ovation's only problem is Drake."

"Do you know how he's doing? Ovation?" Hope and concern mixed in his voice. "I know you and Drake broke up a few months ago, but I haven't heard any updates since spring, when Drake posted that video. I'm sure Clint and Nora would be curious too."

She should've taken more time to check on Ovation when she'd found Rosie and Jasmine grazing nearby. "I think he spends most of his time out in the pasture now, but I'll ask after him the next time I'm out there."

Hollis's eyes narrowed. "Why would you be out there?"

She rubbed her neck as embarrassment oozed over her skin. "He got me some mini cattle when we were dating, but when we broke up, he wouldn't part with them. He doesn't even like them, but he also won't sell them to me. I ... I know I shouldn't be so attached. They're just animals, but ..." She shrugged and gave up the explanation. To continue would've brought on tears, and the situation was already embarrassing enough.

Hollis grunted. "He's a piece of work. Did something similar with Ovation too—wouldn't let me buy him. At least not for a fair market price."

"Well, if I can ask after Ovation for you, something good will come of his insistence on being there when I visit Rosie and Jasmine. Maybe it's the same as with the cows—he's hanging on to him out of spite but otherwise leaves him alone."

The corner of Hollis's mouth pinched. He studied her, his eyes shaded by more than the brim of his hat.

"Anyway." She swiped her palms down her thighs. "That's a dating disaster I don't want to repeat."

"I don't blame you."

"Jack and Dolores do. They're pretty insistent I should be dating, and you're in their crosshairs too. Since I didn't want them pushing us together, I thought it might be best to have a direct conversation with you."

Hollis watched her. Hard man to read.

"The dance ..." She glanced at his arms, the ones she'd been encircled in. At the memory of how secure she'd felt with him, a shiver of something—something a little too like attraction—stirred in her core. She sat straighter, tightening her tummy to smother that traitorous feeling. "It was nice of you to help me out, but that's all the dance was. I'm not dating anyone."

Hollis dipped his chin. "Consider me friend-zoned."

Her stomach knotted. How much deeper could the pit of mortification get?

But then Hollis offered her a hand up in the form of an admission of his own. "I'm more interested in surviving Christmas than anything else."

"I've heard it's rough after a loss." Maybe even rough enough that she shouldn't have said that. She'd lost grandparents, but no one as close to her as everyone said Hollis had been to his father.

Hollis studied his hands. "The first year I was back, Dad was still well enough to go to all the Christmas events around town. But last year, we had to bring the festivities to him. Mom recorded the Christmas play. We had our own cookie decorating contest at home. All that. Not long after, he went downhill, so a lot of my last quality memories of him were this time of year.

"They say to put family first, but nobody really seems to know how to recover from the hole that leaves in your life when they're gone. Not that I regret it. I just ..." He shrugged and shook his head. "I'm not real sure how to carry on."

Drake had never shown such vulnerability.

This insight into Hollis pulled at her allegiances at a much deeper level than attraction had. She *needed* to comfort him, but what could she say that wouldn't seem trite or like she was minimizing his pain?

She straightened her shoulders and tried for a kind smile

that she hoped didn't tiptoe across the line into pity. "I might not be looking to date, but I could always use another friend. If you think it'd help to have company at the events around town, join me and my friends."

"Which events?"

If she was going to keep him away from the Carters—and lead the Carters to believe they didn't need to continue match-making—she and Hollis would need to be together quite a bit. Besides, to cheer him up, more was better, right? "All of them?"

He laughed. "All in, huh?"

"We plan to be at the Christmas play because there's nothing cuter in the world than little kids in costumes with lines they're supposed to remember. Piper and Graham are having a little white elephant Christmas brunch. The gifts are usually pretty useless—they're gag gifts—but Graham's an expert in the kitchen, so you don't want to miss that if you like to eat." She paused, and he nodded to confirm. "And of course, there's the cookie decorating contest. If there's some-thing else you wanted to do, I'm sure we can get a group together."

"Okay. Sure. Why not?"

Really? She hadn't expected this to be so easy. She barely restrained a sigh of relief as she took out her phone. She hesi-tated, peering at the screen. The conversation had gone so well she could tell him the part about introducing him to her single friends too.

But what if that pushed him too far?

She'd take her win and see how it played out before risking any more. "What's your number? I'll text you details about the play."

He recited it, and she texted him her name so he could save her number as well. As soon as he read the message, he turned his screen toward her. "You left off *doctor*. I get to call you Lucy now?"

"My friends do." She rose and stepped toward the door.

Hollis stood as well. "They might get the wrong idea if we spend a lot of time together."

"The Carters? As long as they stop acting on those ideas, they can think whatever they want."

Hollis laughed. "All right. See you at the play."

"See you." She headed back to her truck, relieved.

That really couldn't have gone any better.

Now to become a more subtle matchmaker than Jack and Dolores had been. Then, she'd never have to tell him the rest of the story. A kind and attractive man like Hollis would drum up plenty of interest all on his own, and there were a lot of great women in Redemption Ridge. How hard could it be to set a happily-ever-after in motion?

$$\mathscr{Chapter\ Seven}$$

Hollis lifted his head at the sound of horse hooves approaching. He'd already worked the horses on his roster, but local boarding clients often came out in the evening after work.

Dust Flats, the buckskin mare headed toward him, didn't belong to a local, though. Her owner had driven her in from California for a six-month training program that started a month prior. The man leading the horse out kept the brim of his hat pointed toward the ground, making it difficult to confirm his identity.

"Kurt?" Hollis jogged to the exit, then saw the scene in the drive and stopped.

Kurt was already leading his horse into a waiting trailer.

"What's going on?"

Kurt secured the horse and exited the trailer. Mouth tight, he glanced at Hollis. "Decided to move on."

"You're pulling her from the program?" Dust Flats had been flying through all the early milestones, a fact Hollis had outlined in the regular updates he'd sent to Kurt. "Why?"

Kurt scuffed his boot against the drive. "Just can't take the risk, is all."

"The risk?" Hollis shook his head. Kurt was young—twenty? Twenty-one?—but ranking better each season. He and Dust Flats could make names for themselves together, assuming they had the right foundation. One Hollis had planned to give them.

Kurt swung the trailer door shut and secured the latch. "Ovation isn't even ridable."

The statement hit so hard, Hollis grunted. Drake had posted the video of Ovation throwing him months ago, before Kurt brought Dust Flats to Price Quarter Horses. The only reason for this to be an issue now was if Drake had stirred things up again.

Hollis had asked for it by getting close to Lucy, but what was he supposed to do? Let Drake keep bullying her? He recalled her expression as she'd told him she wasn't interested in dating. He wasn't entirely certain he'd kept his disappointment off his face, but regardless of her desire for a relationship or lack thereof, he'd do whatever it took to keep Drake from hurting her further.

"I've got too much invested in this horse." Kurt pulled his keys from his pocket. "If I wind up with a result like that, it'll ruin me."

A farming family like Kurt's probably didn't have a lot of extra lying around. The horse and its training were a big investment, especially since he hadn't started winning the bigger purses yet.

"Dust Flats isn't like Ovation," Hollis said. "And more importantly, you're not like Drake Hastings. With the right training, Dusty could turn everything around for you. Trust me, she's picking it up quick."

"Yeah, but you said Ovation was good to go too."

Hollis pulsed his jaw. "Ovation came to us head shy and

nervous about being ridden. He had scars on his legs from being worked without boots and wraps. All before he got here." Getting into all of the details he'd shared with Lucy would only dredge up more to debate. Hollis focused on the issue at hand. "I have video that proves we resolved those issues while he was here. Ovation was a solid roping horse before he left."

"And Drake has video from a week later showing he wasn't."

"A lot can happen in a week." Especially when a horse was suffering at the hands of a bad owner. "I offered to buy Ovation from him."

"You backed out after you agreed on a price."

Hollis's anger flared. "We never settled on a price. I offered what the horse was worth fully trained and ready, but Drake Hastings wanted ten grand more than that. We never reached an agreement."

"Not what he says, and the only reason I knew about you offering training is because I've got family in this area. Drake represented one of my cousins after an accident and got him a fair settlement, so ..." Kurt shrugged and retreated toward the cab of his truck. The diesel engine roared, and gravel snapped as the trailer followed the truck away.

Anger pounded against Hollis's ribcage as he watched them go. Was there anything Hastings told the truth about?

"The human's as important as the horse," Dad had said when he taught Hollis to rope. He repeated it again, laughing, when Hollis complained about Dad training horses for Hollis's competitors. And he said it once when he'd declined to take on a rather insistent would-be client.

"I bet you would've seen right through Drake," Hollis said.

Wind stirred, but he didn't take it as an answer from his dad. The man was gone, and no matter how many times he asked for his father's help putting his unfinished business in order, this was all Hollis's problem now.

He put his head down and made his way to the office to try to scrounge up a new training client.

* * *

Rosie and Jasmine waited at the gate for Lucy. Jaz stretched her nose between the rails and lipped a banana from her hand. Rosie pushed in too, and Lucy had to surrender the second banana before they backed up enough to allow her to enter.

"You do spoil them."

Her stomach knotted at Drake's voice behind her. She hated his supervision, and she wasn't sure how to bring up Ovation without raising suspicion. Even lingering near the fence for a chat with Drake would be unusual enough to wave a red flag.

She brandished the comb she'd brought. "And it's about to get worse."

Highland cattle didn't need grooming, but Rosie and Jasmine seemed to enjoy being brushed out. She spent about twenty minutes in the pasture with them before returning to the gate. Drake delivered a fresh hay bale, so Lucy refilled the water trough.

He finished first and stopped beside her. "I'm surprised your boyfriend lets you come out here."

He must mean Hollis. Not having to deal with Drake alone at the dance had been nice, but he could be nasty when someone else got something he wanted. Besides, if one of her biggest complaints about Drake was his habitual lies, she ought to tell the truth. "Hollis and I aren't together."

His eyebrows lifted. "Are you sure you don't want to talk to him first? Get your stories straight?"

She shook her head, not following and afraid to ask.

Drake eyed her. "I had a talk with him after the barn dance."

And Hollis hadn't said anything? How could he send her into this conversation blind?

"I don't know what you're thinking." Drake motioned to the cows. "You're all about the animals, yet you're with a man who'd traumatize a horse? You saw for yourself how Ovation turned out."

Clearly, he didn't believe her about Hollis. Arguing with him about such a thing seemed ridiculous. Besides, the conversation had led where she wanted it to—Ovation. "I saw the video. But if the horse is as bad as all that, why do you still have him?"

"Been busy at work, so I turned him out, but a day of reckoning is coming. I can't keep charity cases forever."

Hollis would likely still be happy to buy Ovation, but she kept that to herself. The deal had fallen through last time, and Drake showed no signs of being more cooperative now.

Drake peered toward Rosie and Jasmine.

And then it hit her. He'd spoken in the plural just now—charity cases, not *a* charity case. Her stomach dropped like she'd been thrown from a bull. He'd once joked about Highland cattle meat tasting like bison. Would he have the animals—Rosie, Jasmine, and Ovation—slaughtered to keep them away from Hollis and Lucy?

Surely, he'd announce that intention first to lord his power over them. Right?

Tears pressed on her eyes. She wanted to run back into the field and wrap her arms around Rosie and Jasmine, but they nosed around the pasture, mercifully oblivious. If she got close, they might pick up on her panic. Besides, the only way away from Drake was to leave his property.

Maybe she ought to stop her visits here, but for all she

knew, the only reason he'd kept the cows alive this long was because of her.

She held her head up, slowed her breathing, and met Drake's glare. She'd pay thousands of dollars to have the right thing to say to him. Something biting that would put him in his place. All she managed was confident posture as she said, "I'll see you next time."

Chapter Eight

Hollis checked Lucy's text, then headed up the outside aisle in the elementary school auditorium toward where he should find her and her friends. Conversations hummed, and children darted around, passing the time until the play would start. He waved to Clint, but the guy was too busy chatting with Nora to notice. Typical.

Tonight marked the first time in Hollis's adult life he'd attended the annual play of his own volition. Any other time he'd come, he'd been talked into it by his parents, who enjoyed the antics of the pint-sized actors. Afterward, Mom would inevitably make some comment alluding to a desire for grandchildren. Dad used to pat her hand and say something like, "Let's not put the carriage before the horse."

Mom would then turn her questions to the horse—his love life. He'd dated some, but never found someone he could envision forever with, and when Mom would question that, Dad would point out that they didn't want him marrying just anyone.

At the time, Hollis had appreciated the space his dad had given him.

Now, he regretted things hadn't worked out differently. Dad might've been laid-back about it, but he'd wanted grand-children too, and he'd never get the chance to meet them. Assuming either he or Will ever managed to settle down and have kids of their own.

"Hollis! Over here!" Lucy called from behind.

He'd walked right by where she sat with her friends. She grinned and motioned him over with enthusiasm that stopped his spiraling thoughts. Reversed them, actually. This was just a friendship, but some friendships grew into more. Just look at Clint and Nora. For years, they'd sworn they'd never be more than friends. Now the two were so good together, Hollis couldn't help a twinge of envy.

Piper and Graham moved to the aisle to let him into the row, while Lucy stood and tucked herself as close as possible to her seat. Even so, it was hard not to invade her space on his way to the empty chair. Her verdant perfume—wisps of which had hung in the office after she'd left—greeted him. Out of respect for other audience members, most people had left their hats behind, so her hair spilled unencumbered around her face and shoulders.

"Hollis, have you met Neenah?" She swept a hand toward the woman on his other side.

With good posture and her dark hair back in a no-nonsense ponytail, Neenah had an almost military bearing. He'd heard Cody mention a coworker named Neenah but hadn't met her before.

He nodded hello. "Nice to meet you."

She offered a brief smile. "Lucy's been telling me about you."

"Oh?" He glanced Lucy's way. "Good things or bad?"

Lucy pointed him back to Neenah. "Neenah is a police officer, but you two have rodeo in common."

"I was a trick rider, but I quit when I finished college."

Despite her short stature, Neenah's voice was low. "Police work is all the adrenaline rush I need."

"I bet. Not an easy line of work."

"It runs in her blood. Right, Neenah?" Lucy bumped his arm as she leaned to see around him.

She gave a curt nod. "My father and brothers are all cops too, back in Wyoming where I'm from."

"Hollis followed his dad in his career too. Another thing you have in common."

He managed the requisite smile, but why was it so important to Lucy that he and Neenah find common ground? Was this simply small talk?

Before the awkwardness could continue, the lights dimmed, and a spotlight focused on the stage. The principal gave an introduction, and a flurry of snowflake-dressed kiddos fluttered onto the stage to begin the production.

* * *

Matchmaking wasn't so hard. Lucy had already made the introduction between Hollis and Neenah, and with another little nudge, their relationship would be on its way.

When the play ended and Hollis turned toward her, he motioned at Graham and Piper's empty seats. "Where'd they go?"

"Their nephew, Bryce, was babysitting, but he couldn't get the baby to settle, so they left." Lucy smirked. "You must've really been into the performance to not notice."

Which, come to think of it, was kind of endearing. Then a cold thought blew through. Hollis may have been preoccupied with Neenah, not the kids. A shiver shimmied down her arms before she could convince herself that was what she'd wanted.

Hollis shot a grin at the stage. "If they ducked out somewhere around the time when the snowman shouted to ask his mom if he could have cake when he got home, yeah, I was pretty invested."

Lucy chuckled and followed his gaze, but all the little actors were already in the crowd with their parents, headed home to bed. Or cake. "Some parents shouldn't come up front to get pictures."

"The kids might stay in character, but would that really be better?" Humor rumbled in his voice, and what she wouldn't give to coax him into laughter.

"Fair point."

"Excuse me." Neenah's voice rose from beyond Hollis, reminding Lucy of her responsibility. How had she gotten so caught up in chatting with him that she'd forgotten already?

She stepped into the aisle. "You two want to go get nachos or something? It's still early."

"Can't. I have a shift to get to." With the matter-of-fact statement, Neenah waved and headed off with the departing crowd.

So much for Lucy's plan to get Hollis and Neenah to El Cresta, the Mexican place on the square, and then bail early, leaving them to get to know each other. Disappointed, she stepped back into the row to check under her seat for anything she might've dropped or forgotten.

"What are you two crazy kids up to?"

Lucy straightened at the all-too-cheerful voice. Dolores Carter stood in the aisle, her hand clamped around Hollis's forearm. Her husband was beside her, Lucy's parents and Hollis's mom behind her.

"Sounds like we're getting nachos." Hollis glanced at Lucy and then surveyed the little crowd they'd collected. "You're welcome to join—"

"Oh, we couldn't possibly intrude, dear." Dolores scrunched her nose.

Lucy's parents studied Hollis, but Lucy could clear things

up with them later. The curiosity on Susan's face, however, warranted immediate intervention. "Of course you could join us. It's not a date or anything."

"You know us old folk." Dolores released his arm. "It's getting close to bedtime, and none of us like driving after dark."

Even Mom and Dad didn't object, though seven o'clock was nowhere near their bedtime and neither of them much minded driving at night—an inescapable task, since the sun set before the show even started. They filed away after the Carters, and only Susan cast a second look backward. The assurances about the casual nature of their plans hadn't doused her curiosity, evidently.

"Shall we?" Hollis lifted a hand toward the exit.

Lucy felt as wobbly and worried as the kids on stage had looked when they forgot their lines. She couldn't explain that she'd never intended to stay for nachos, because that would mean admitting she'd been trying to set him up with Neenah. So, she found herself nodding.

A buzz of excitement at the one-on-one time flitted through her chest—only to be squashed by the realization she ought to use the time to catch him up on what Drake had said. Her stomach still churned every time she wondered what he'd meant about a day of reckoning.

Twenty minutes later, they waited at the hostess station. Others must've had the same idea about getting food after the play, because the place was unusually busy for the time of evening in a small town.

A family bustled in and got in line behind them.

Hollis did a double take, then turned toward the father with his hand extended. "Hey, Weston, how's it going?"

"Good. Good." Weston's drawn eyebrows told a different story. "You?"

"I've been trying to reach you. I've got an opening. We can

get to work on Honeybear, have her in shape for this spring for you."

Weston's wife diverted her gaze to her children and intervened when the older boy mussed his brother's hair.

"I got the messages. Here's the thing ... It's not gonna work out this time." Weston cringed. "Real sorry. You understand?"

"You were excited about the program and the results we get. What changed?"

Lucy tensed. She'd never have the guts to pose the question, though it was completely fair and Hollis had asked in a curious, friendly tone.

"It's ... it's, ah ..." Weston ran the back of his fingers along his jawline. "It's a real big investment. I have a young family. Have to be smart, and that's a big risk."

"Okay." Hollis's mouth tightened, but he dipped his head. "Thanks for letting me know. I'll go to the next name on the list."

"Sure thing." The other man bit his lip, then forced a smile. "Thanks for understanding."

Hollis turned back. From behind him, the other family probably couldn't see him working his jaw, but Lucy noticed. He also stood a little too still. But she couldn't ask about it with the problem standing right behind them, so they all awkwardly ignored each other until finally a booth was ready, and the hostess led Lucy and Hollis away.

Lucy immediately leaned over the lacquered tabletop. "What was that about?"

Hollis sat back and rested his hands on his lap. "I had a client suddenly quit the training program. I've been reaching out to people who expressed an interest, trying to fill the spot." His eyes narrowed like he was thinking. "When that client quit, he talked about investment and risk a lot like

Weston did just now. So did one of the other owners I talked to."

"I can see training being an investment, but a risk? Why would they all have that idea?"

"Drake." Hollis's low tone snapped with frustration. "I know at least one of them talked to him. Given the similarities, he's making the rounds."

Lucy's shoulders dropped. Then she remembered what Drake said early in her conversation with him, before she'd gotten so distracted by the idea of something bad befalling her cows. "I hear he talked to you at some point after the barn dance?"

Hollis stilled, watching her. "He did."

"And you told him we were together?"

"No. I just didn't correct him."

Lucy hugged one arm across herself. She'd gone along with the charade at the dance, so she could hardly blame him for letting it continue. "He's the type to pounce on anything, and a fake relationship is too tempting of a target."

"I'd rather be a target than a pushover. And I'd definitely rather have him bothering me than you." Protectiveness flashed in his eyes.

Lucy had thought him attractive before. Now, she sat on her hands to keep from reaching out to borrow strength from his reassuring grip. "That's sweet, but I can't avoid him, and he's more intolerable if he sniffs a lie. I told him we're not together. I don't know if he believed me, but ..."

The server interrupted to get their drink orders. Lucy ordered loaded nachos right away to cut down on further interruptions.

Once they were alone again, she refocused on Hollis. "I did ask after Ovation."

He looked up, wary hope lifting his features.

"He has him in a pasture—alone, unfortunately—but at

least he's not being mistreated. Drake did say he can't keep charity cases forever. I'm worried about that."

Hollis's jaw pulsed again. "If he offloads Ovation, I'll snatch him up."

"If he gives you the chance."

Hollis scoffed. "He's no fool. He'll sell to whoever will give him the most money, and that's me."

His confidence bolstered Lucy's own hopes. Perhaps they could sway Drake from any disastrous plan with money. Unfortunately, buying Highland cattle would wipe out her meager savings account. She might even need to take out a loan—if the bank would give her more, considering what she already owed.

The server brought their drinks and moved on to check on another table.

Lucy fiddled with her straw wrapper. "How does Drake know who your clients are to scare them away?"

"Weston's local, and the other client he scared off was related to someone Drake represented. But he's working beyond that too. I've come across some new posts he wrote about Ovation in online forums, the type of places where people go to get opinions. I don't know a lot of these guys personally, so they choose a trainer based on reputation."

Now her protective streak flared. "Price Quarter Horses are proven winners."

"We've still got good bloodlines, and some people will buy horses from us based on that alone, but without training clients, we won't be able to make ends meet for long. Unfortunately, on that front, I was just a kid when Dad started Pepperjack. I had very little involvement training Manny and none with Cam."

She'd heard the names many times from Chantal and others—including announcers of televised rodeos. "The horses you rode when Pepperjack got older."

"Our most famous successes."

"But they're famous thanks to you." Roping horses like Hollis's needed a sense of when to go, where to run, and how much tension to maintain after a calf was on the line. As an animal lover, Lucy liked to watch the mounts, but she must've been in the minority, because camera crews often cut the horse out of the shot after the cowboy dismounted to tie down the calf. Though she'd been frustrated by the tunnel vision in the past, that focus on the rider ought to help Hollis now.

"Maybe so, but they showcase my dad's ability as a trainer, not mine. Dad did spend his last good year training me in his methods, but the whole world didn't see that. The only skill I've widely proven is I can tie down a calf in under eight seconds—given the right horse. None of the horses I trained over last winter racked up big wins during this year's rodeo season. Even if one of them had, one winner isn't much of a track record."

"So Drake's quite a problem." She bit the inside of her cheek. Why had she gotten involved with that awful man? And when would she and those she cared about be free of his terrible influence?

"He wouldn't be, if Dad were still around." The quiet statement plucked her heartstrings.

"How so?"

"Longer track record, and people wanted to train under him. He built that big barn so he could head up a whole team. More trainers would've meant more clients, and more clients mean more revenue to pay for said barn. But he got sick before he could make it happen. No one wants to train under me— maybe for roping lessons, but not on how to train a horse."

"You could bring in someone more experienced."

"Dad was the best in the business. Experts like that are content where they're at or they're looking for more money than the ranch can spare." His discouragement was almost palpable.

She prayed the Lord would show her the silver lining so she could point it out to Hollis. All she could think of was that big, beautiful stable. "There must be other ways to put the barn to use."

"We fill the stalls with boarding clients and earn something off exercising the ones the owners can't get to regularly, but that's less income than training clients. Same with teaching roping seminars. Doesn't make ends meet."

"So, buying Ovation ..."

Hollis nodded. "It'd take a hunk of what's left of my savings, but what I have isn't enough to save the ranch anyway. Might as well use it to give Ovation a better future."

Her nose stung. The situation at Price Quarter Horses was that dire? "The ranch has been in your family for generations." Not to mention Hollis had been a top roper. Those guys earned huge payouts and sponsorships.

"Dad borrowed against the ranch to invest in a scheme my ... in a real estate flip that was supposed to be a sure thing. I invested too. It was family, so ..." Lines bracketed his mouth. "Unfortunately, it fell through. Since Dad already had the equity in the land tied up, he got the money for the barn and other improvements from private investors. His plan was to have the business in good shape so he'd qualify for a traditional loan before the private loans came due next summer. But he failed to plan for cancer."

"I'm sorry."

The server set a platter of nachos in the center of the table and two plates beside it. Hollis handed one to Lucy and took the other for himself. The chips were coated in cheese, pico de gallo, jalapenos, and more, and the savory scent was undeniably appetizing, but it felt wrong to eat in the face of Hollis's situation.

"Sounds like family stuff has been really hard for a few years now. First the investment, then cancer, now the ranch ..." She probably shouldn't be rubbing it in by naming everything, so she trailed to a stop.

"But what do we have if we don't have family, right?"

"Sounds like you and your mom are still close?"

He dipped his head. "And for all the difficulty, if there were something more I could give to make this easier for her, I would do it."

She believed him, and her throat turned scratchy with emotion. It sounded to her like he was a kindred spirit, someone who would do anything for loved ones. If only dedication and sacrifice were more reliable predictors of positive outcomes.

He motioned for her to serve herself, then used his fork to scoop a helping from the platter to his own plate. "Enough about the ranch. Tell me about your practice."

"Well, like you, I've got a lot of loans to keep up with. So, instead of buying a building, I've rented an office that's mostly just for paperwork and I do my business out in the field. In large part because of Jack Carter, I've been able to make it work. He sold me a bunch of used equipment at a steal, referred a number of clients to me, and still consults if I'm stumped on a case. Thanks to him, someday I might even be able to pay off school and all my equipment."

Hollis chuckled, as she'd intended him to. "You've known him a long time?"

"He and Dolores have been friends of my parents going back before I was born."

"Is he the one who inspired you to get into veterinary medicine?"

"Indirectly." She chewed her lip and debated continuing, but Hollis had shared plenty of personal details. She might as well reciprocate. "When I was a girl, a cow on a neighboring farm had a hard delivery. My dad went over to help, and I tagged along. Things didn't go well. Both the calf and cow died."

Hollis winced.

"I was eleven. Old enough to know what Jack did for a living, that he could've saved both the cow and calf, but I guess for that farmer, things were tight. The cost of a C-section would've been higher than the cost of replacing the livestock. It seemed incredibly unfair to me that a choice like that would have to come down to money and skill. I couldn't understand why Dad didn't call Jack to help, why Jack wouldn't have come to do it, even without pay, if it meant saving lives."

"Cow lives." Hollis's smirk died. "Then again, you have a thing for cows, don't you?"

"If you met Rosie and Jasmine, you'd understand. They're like great big, goofy dogs."

"I think the same thing about Pep sometimes." He smiled. "I'm game to meet them."

Drake would throw a fit. He already put Hollis down any chance he got. She refocused on her story. "I know now livestock is more of a financial investment than an emotional one. I've come to terms with that. But back then, I didn't see a difference between pets and livestock. I threw such a fit about it, Dad had to drag me back to the truck, struggling and sobbing. I hated feeling that helpless, so I learned how to take care of animals. I rescued tadpoles from a puddle. I nursed a dehydrated chipmunk back to health—"

"A what?"

"He got trapped in our garage during a heat wave. I found him collapsed on the floor, too weak to run away. I nursed him back to health and set him free again. There was a whole string of wildlife. I also studied up on how to best help cows and horses with difficult births. Once I got my driver's license, I worked at Jack's clinic until I went off to college, and I interned with him over summers."

"And now no animal has to die on your watch."

"I wish that were the case. Unfortunately, death is part of the deal."

"How do you ..." Hollis rolled his lips in, sighed, and tried again. "I mean, it sounds like you're pretty invested in your work, so how do you cope with that side of the job?"

"I'd like to think I've grown up since age eleven." She laughed, but his expression fell. He must've hoped for a real answer, not a deflection. She tried again. "I take comfort in knowing that I've done the best I can to give them healthy, quality lives and as good of an end as possible. Death is part of the curse, but I believe that God will one day make all things right. I don't entirely know what that means in the case of animals, but I do know God is good, and I'm trusting them to Him."

Hollis nodded, eyes focused on the table. Thinking of his father, perhaps? He glanced up at her, forced a smile, sat up straighter. "We're going to have to talk about lighter subjects if we ever want to eat anything."

The cheese on the nachos was already cooling, so Lucy changed the subject, though what she really wanted to do was go around the table, slide onto the bench with Hollis, wrap him in a hug, and tell him she was sorry for his loss and that everything would turn out all right.

Did a friend get to do that?

Maybe.

Or maybe it'd blur the neat lines she'd drawn to keep from repeating the mistakes she'd made with Drake. After all, she hadn't known Hollis any longer than she'd known her ex before getting involved with him. She couldn't be trusted to spot a bad one, even when he was just an arm's length away, peering at her with kind blue eyes and laughing at her jokes.

To keep herself from falling for him, she absolutely needed to set him up with someone else.

The sooner, the better.

Chapter Nine

The rope between the saddle horn and the log tightened. Hollis dismounted and hit the ground running. Fontina, a seven-year-old mare born and bred at Price Quarter Horses, continued backing up as Hollis approached the log she was pulling. When he sat on the log, she stopped and kept tension on the line.

Their training was paying off.

He waited a few seconds then remounted and ran the exercise again. Eventually, the horse would get a feel for when to back up and when to hold the line, even if a calf, not a log, tugged at the end of the rope.

Hollis's mom stepped into the indoor training arena and took a seat on a bench by the door. She didn't attempt to flag him down, so he put Fontina through the drill a few more times before having her drag the log back to where they stored it. Free of the weight, he cooled her down with a slow lap around the arena.

"Tough session?" Mom asked as they drew near.

"Not at all." He dismounted one last time. "Why?"

She tucked her feet back under the bench, then swung

them forward and popped to a stand. "If a session went well, your father always had this look about him as he wrapped up. Stood a little taller, smiled a little easier. You ..." She studied him, and he felt like a teenager again, hoping she couldn't guess the no good he'd been up to.

But what did he have to hide? The answer hit him like a hoof to the jaw. The ranch's books.

"You look weighed down."

"It's been a long year."

They exited the arena. Fontina's clopping hooves kept time behind them until they reached the grooming stall by the tack room. Hollis swapped out the bridle for a halter and clipped the horse to the cross ties.

"You know when you looked lighter?" Mom started on the saddle without him asking. He might've kept the books from her, and she left training to his dad and now him, but she helped in most other functions around the ranch. "During that dance."

Hollis rested a hand on Fontina's shoulder and lowered his face.

"Don't you roll your eyes at me, young man."

He hadn't, but thanks to his hat and the horse, she couldn't see his eyes. Something told him she wouldn't take much kindlier to the way he'd jammed them shut. "Why is everyone suddenly concerned about whether I'm dating?"

"Everyone?"

"Jack and Dolores tried to set me up with Lucy."

"You say that like they failed."

"As Lucy puts it, I could always use another friend. But we're not dating." He lifted the saddle off and stowed it on the saddle rack.

Mom fell silent as they groomed Fontina, but she stuck close, even as he turned the mare out into a paddock.

He felt like he was being stalked by a mountain lion. No,

something friendlier than that. A golden retriever, maybe. "I've got some more work to do, so don't wait on me for dinner, okay?"

She lifted an eyebrow. "Family dinners have always been a priority around here."

Except the family had dwindled to the two of them, and their losses were never more evident than when they sat at the table and ignored the empty seats. Then again, Will wasn't at the table because he chose not to come home. Hollis couldn't compound that pain by leaving his own seat empty too.

Still, there was no shortage of work to do in the barn if he was somehow going to turn this financial situation around. Was Lucy on to something regarding his reputation in rodeo? How could he better leverage that? If he came up with a plan, he'd feel a lot more comfortable around Mom. "Can I have an hour?"

"Sure thing."

He stepped away, on course for the tack he'd left in the grooming stall.

"Do you like it?" Mom asked.

He turned back. "Like what?"

"The work. Training. Ranching."

"It's in my blood."

"And cancer was in your dad's bones. Just because something's a part of you doesn't mean it's good for you."

He gaped at her. How could she equate the work they did here with cancer? Did she not want him here? Not care what became of the family business? "I don't like how some situations have played out, but that doesn't mean I'm in the wrong place. Family is everything."

"Family is a blessing that comes from God, but only God is everything."

He sighed. "It's a turn of speech."

She tipped her head. "Only God won't let you down."

Now he looked away. Swallowed hard. Hollis certainly felt let down by his dad's death and by the ranch's finances, both of which God could have changed.

Mom must have read his doubts in his expression because she continued. "I know in the face of some things, it doesn't seem that way. But during those seasons, we can look back on ways we've seen God's faithfulness in the past—in our own lives, in Scripture—and choose faith, no matter what our circumstances are telling us." She looked wistfully around, and her voice lowered. "God is good, son."

"He is." The words grated against his raw throat. He knew them to be true. He just had trouble reconciling them with the losses they faced. That was what faith was for, he supposed. But it didn't have to be blind faith. That was why she'd encouraged him to reflect on past provision. He had to acknowledge he had lived an uncommon life, stuffed full of blessings from rodeo success to being raised on this beautiful ranch by two parents who loved him. "Thanks, Mom."

She gave a little smile and started for the house. She was a few stalls away when her voice reached him again. "By the way, Will's coming home for Christmas."

Frustration tackled the peace he'd felt just moments ago.

"He arrives tonight." Her voice held a warning.

She wanted Hollis on his best behavior. Thanks to Will, he always had to be. If both Price brothers ran around unconcerned about their impact on the world around them, they'd have lost this place already.

* * *

On Saturday morning, Lucy stopped at The Cakery on her way to the gift exchange breakfast at Piper and Graham's. After all, what was a big brunch spread without scones?

Caroline Taylor, the head baker, was loading cupcakes into

the display case. She finished before the cashier boxed up another customer's order and smiled at Lucy. "What can I get you?"

"The cranberry scones look amazing." Lucy pointed at the glaze-drizzled triangles.

"Just made a fresh batch this morning. How many do you need?"

Lucy counted off the usual suspects on her fingers—Graham, Piper, Bryce, Cody, Lucy, and Neenah. Plus, of course, Hollis. "Ten, please." That way there'd be enough if someone wanted seconds or, more likely considering the amount of food Graham was probably cooking up, she would get to take some home with her.

"Comin' up." Caroline deftly folded a pastry box and nestled scones inside. "Anything exciting going on these days?"

The only thing—or person, rather—that came to mind was Hollis. Hollis, listening as she rambled about that cow from her childhood. Hollis, talking about his father with so much respect and admiration. Hollis, determined to carry on the legacy in the face of adversity.

The same Hollis she was trying to set up with someone else. Anyone else.

Not the sort of thing she could drop into a quick chat with an acquaintance, even if Caroline was just about the sweetest human in Redemption Ridge.

"I'm staying busy with work and just about every Christmas activity the town has to offer."

Caroline laughed. "I thought I saw you at the play. And the barn dance. What's on the docket for this morning?"

"White elephant gift exchange with friends."

"Oh, what're you bringing? Aside from scones, of course." Caroline fit the lid into place and set the box on the counter.

Lucy carried it over to the register. "The gifts are supposed to be gag gifts, so I wrapped up a pig-shaped planter. I got it from a client and felt obligated to use it for a while, but it's faded from the sun now, so off he goes."

"Sounds fun, but ..." As the cashier went to help another customer, Caroline leaned closer. "When I asked about anything exciting, I was thinking of all the time I hear you're spending with a certain former rodeo star?"

"Oh, Hollis?" She shook her head, perhaps a bit more enthusiastically than strictly required. "I'm not dating anyone. Even former rodeo stars."

In fact, if Lucy failed to nudge Hollis and Neenah together, perhaps she should see what she could do about introducing him to Caroline. She was pretty, as sweet as they came, and if her tone was any indication, she thought Hollis was a catch.

"How about you?" Lucy asked. "Seeing anyone?"

"No. Life is so full with family, friends, and of course my work here." With a flourish, she indicated the picture-perfect sweets filling the displays. She punched a few buttons and pointed to the total.

Lucy tapped her card to pay. "But if the right guy came along ..."

"I hope someday he does—for both you and me." Caroline chuckled and passed her the receipt.

As Lucy left the shop and continued toward Graham and Piper's house, she thought back through the last few years. She hadn't heard of Caroline dating anyone, at least not for very long, so a broken heart or bad experience probably hadn't caused her reluctance to date.

Maybe the right guy hadn't come along yet, or maybe she just needed the right introduction. Caroline was a couple of years younger than Lucy, so maybe eight or so years younger than Hollis, but that wasn't a big enough difference to make things weird, right? Either way, Lucy saw Penelope at Bethany's

Book Barn setting up a display about age-gap romances the last time she'd been out to the bookstore. If it was good enough for romance novels, it was good enough for real life, right?

Lucy let herself into Piper and Graham's house, and the dogs charged over, barking.

"Banjo. Teddy." Graham clapped, and the graying black Lab, Banjo, returned to his master. Teddy, their Goldendoodle, bounced his nose against the bottom of the gift-wrapped box with the planter inside.

Lucy held it steady, so the scones stacked on top didn't slide. Bryce, Piper's twelve-year-old nephew who lived with the couple, led Teddy away by the collar. Graham took the load from her.

"Thank you." She transferred the scones to the table, and Graham added the white elephant gift to the pile of colorfully wrapped boxes that must contain the family's contributions to the exchange.

They'd decorated for Christmas since the last time she'd been here. Lights winked on the tree in the corner, and a festive tablecloth covered the table. A banner that read "O, come let us adore Him" in gold foil hung on the wall.

Piper entered with Jasper in the crook of her elbow and greeted Lucy with a one-armed hug. Meanwhile, Graham and Bryce disappeared into the kitchen.

Lucy pointed after them. "Do they need any help?"

"Just take a seat," Graham called. "Everything's ready and staying warm in the oven."

Lucy surveyed the table. There was an extra seat and no good way to guarantee Hollis ended up by Neenah. Lucy chose the place across from Piper's seat on one end. That would at least make sure they weren't on complete opposite sides.

Moments later, Neenah and Cody entered. When they

made it to the table, they chose seats on the same side as Piper and Graham's.

"I feel like I'm here for a panel or something," Lucy quipped.

Neenah's eyes narrowed playfully. "Not at all. This is an interrogation."

"A what? Why?"

Cody cocked his head. "Is it just me, or does she sound guilty?"

Piper's eyes danced. "That's our Lucy, always up to no good."

Lucy scoffed. "That's not fair. Name one time."

Graham appeared, carrying a quiche with hot mitts. "How about when you suddenly got too busy to help at Second Chances and cornered me into working the Black Friday shift?"

Even before Lucy had backed out of her commitment at Piper's charming secondhand shop two years ago, Graham had been spending a lot of time there to prepare a donation for a benefit auction. Still, his and Piper's relationship had been tenuous, thanks to a falling out years before that.

"As I recall, you two got engaged less than ... what, two months after that shift together? You should be thanking me."

Piper lifted Jasper's hand, waved it at her, and faked a baby voice. "Thank you for playing matchmaker."

"Ew." Bryce's lip curled as he set a steaming bowl of hash browns on the table.

"There's *more* matchmaking going on?" Hollis's voice broadcast from near the front door.

Lucy's tingling guilt suggested she *did* deserve the interrogation her friends had teased about. How had she missed the door opening?

The dogs raced from the kitchen and charged him, sparing

her having to reply. Hopefully, no one else put much stock into what he'd said.

Hollis half-greeted, half-herded the dogs back so he could step farther in, allowing another man through the door. The latest guest's face so resembled Hollis's, she did a double take. But no, his eyes were brown, not blue, and his features were more rounded. She'd seen him around over the years, just not often or recently.

"You all know my brother Will?" Hollis's voice was gruff as he added two gift bags to the collection. "He's home for Christmas. I ran into Graham yesterday, and he said, 'the more the merrier,' so ..."

Will nodded a greeting, unable to wave because of the two foil-wrapped plates he held. "We stopped by the fire department's fundraiser breakfast for bacon and pancakes."

"Thanks. Any open space on the table's fine." Graham disappeared back into the kitchen.

Hollis pointed to each person, rattling off names. Meanwhile, Graham returned with pitchers of orange juice and water. Bryce took a seat, hungrily eying the food, so Lucy followed Graham back to the kitchen to help. Sure enough, a coffee cake, a plate of sausages, and a jug of milk all waited to be carried in.

Piper appeared at her elbow. "What does Hollis mean about *more* matchmaking? He doesn't know about me and Graham, right?"

She mashed her lips together. "Jack and Dolores Carter got some ideas. I guess they'd like to see Hollis find someone."

Piper's eyebrows lifted. "Someone in particular?"

"From what Dolores said, no, she's not very particular." Lucy scooped up the milk and sausages and fled back to the dining table.

The Price brothers had chosen chairs beside hers, Hollis

thankfully across from Neenah, and Will next to Lucy. She set the dishes on the table and approached her chair.

Will pulled it out for her. "My lady." He winked.

The flirtation would be wasted on Lucy. She was immune to charm, thanks to Drake. But if Will stayed focused on her, he wouldn't interfere between Hollis and Neenah. So, Lucy chuckled and let him tuck the seat in behind her.

* * *

Hollis watched as Will pulled a plastic animal from the box. About a foot and a half tall and faded pink with triangle-shaped ears, Hollis mistook it for a dog until he saw the distinctive snout. That explained the color. The pig had a hole in his back shaped like a flowerpot. An outdoor planter, apparently.

"Okay, who brought this masterpiece?" Will held the thing beside his face like he was posing for a selfie.

The three cops in attendance—Cody, Graham, and Neenah—had each shown impressive poker faces at various times throughout their breakfast, but all three smiled now. Piper shot a furtive glance at Lucy, who appeared to be biting her lips together.

Jealousy stirred. Of course Will had been the one to open her gift. As if the guy needed another opportunity to hit on her.

Will's scan of the room stopped on her. "Was it you?"

She opened her mouth, hesitated a moment too long, and said, "Why would you ask that?"

"It *was* you." Will's tone was as warm and sweet as the syrup served with breakfast, and it made Hollis ill. "What's his name?"

"Mud."

"Mud? His name is Mud?" Will laughed like he'd never

heard a funnier joke. "Welcome to the family, Mud." He thumped the pig's side, and it resounded like a drum.

"Don't welcome her just yet." Piper pointed to Hollis, who'd drawn the highest number.

Because of it, he was the only person who had yet to claim a gift. According to the rules, he could either take a gift someone else had opened earlier or he could take the remaining unopened present.

Will shot him a smug smile. "Oh, Holly Boy won't take a pig. He had a bad experience."

He was going there while in slugging distance? Hollis clenched a fist. It was bad enough Will had caused the worst of the ranch's financial situation and acted like he hadn't a care in the world. Now he wanted to test if the childhood nickname and the pig incident would be the straw that broke Hollis's restraint?

Well, not in front of Lucy.

Not ever. The thought sounded an awful lot like Dad.

Hollis claimed the last box. Sure, he'd rather not let Will take any piece of Lucy, even a discarded planter, but taking Will's bait by fighting for the planter would come at a cost. If Will thought he was upsetting Hollis by showering Lucy with attention, he'd double down.

This was already bad enough.

Beneath the wrapping, the box Hollis had claimed was coated in duct tape. He worked his knife from his pocket and cut it open to find a layer of bubble wrap. He moved that aside and found more bubble wrap. And more, all layered in flat sheets, one after another. As he pulled them out, sheet after sheet, the laughter in the room grew. Finally, he got to the bottom of the box. Nothing there.

"I believe I just got my very own supply of bubble wrap." He picked up two fistfuls and held them up for Neenah. As the first to go, she had the option of stealing at the end. "Interested?"

"I'm good, thanks." She hugged her bag of chocolate closer. "Except I do want to hear about this bad experience."

"Oh, good choice." Will clapped him on the shoulder. "You wanna tell it, or should I?"

"I'm sure you remember it more clearly than I do, since I was all of four years old at the time."

"Four, and yet so independent he wandered off from the family at a huge rodeo and stock show, and he winds up in the livestock barn." Hand still heavy on Hollis's shoulder, Will motioned a wide circle with his other arm like he was inviting everyone to envision a far-off and fantastical land.

His spell-casting seemed to work. Even pre-teen Bryce, who'd started for his room, had stopped by the door to listen.

"I'm, like, thirteen, and Mom and Dad don't want me out of their sight—they already had one son wander off, after all, and Mom's about two seconds from notifying the authorities —but I'm sprinting ahead, looking for my kid brother." Will released Hollis to mime a frantic search. "Where do I find him? In a stall with a sow and her litter, and let me tell you, *that* Mud was none too happy about it."

Hollis rubbed his mouth. He should've told the story himself to cut down on the theatrics. "I was *four*," he muttered.

Will ignored him. "The pig backed him up against the side of the stall with a headbutt, and she had her head all low and menacing, snapping her teeth. There was Hollis, trying to reach the top of the stall wall, but it was made up of vertical bars, so who knows how he got in there in the first place, but one thing was for sure. He wasn't gonna climb his way out. So good news is, I'm older and big enough to reach over and pull him out just in time for that crazy sow to plow right into the bars, shaking the whole stall. Hasn't liked a pig he's met since."

Hollis had gotten a far more important takeaway from the story. That day's events had taught him to stick by family. If only something had happened to teach Will the same. But a lighthearted Christmas party wasn't the time for a discussion like that, so he rolled with Will's tone. "Maybe not one I've met, but I've had plenty of delicious pork over the years."

The quip earned a round of laughter.

"Good news." Lucy's lips tipped in a kind smile. "I think I'm the only one here who regularly interacts with pigs, so planter aside, you're in fairly safe company. Piper and Graham like dogs ... Cody, do you like any animals?"

"Not enough to own one."

Lucy's circle of the room continued. "And Neenah is a fellow horse lover. You two should go for a trail ride sometime." She pointed between him and Neenah.

Neenah's eyebrows tented with curious surprise. Cody crossed his arms and cocked his head with an assessing gaze on Lucy. Piper pressed a hand over a grin.

"What?" Lucy lifted her hands, apparently noticing the same range of reactions Hollis had. She focused on Hollis. "She got her horse from your dad just a few years ago. It'd be a reunion of sorts. BeeBee might really enjoy seeing her old family and friends—horses remember those things. There are studies."

Piper dropped both her hand and the goofy grin. One vote for believing Lucy had no alternative motive. Cody still watched Lucy, though.

"BeeBee?" Will asked. "That's a type of cheese?"

If the horse had come from Price Quarter Horses during Dad's run, it must be. He'd worked through the more common cheeses early on, so he'd had to get more creative as time passed.

Neenah nodded. "Officially, she's Beenleigh Blue, named after a blue cheese because she's a blue roan."

Hollis rubbed the center of his chest. That color had been a favorite of Dad's.

"They make blue horses?" Piper's voice went high with doubt.

Hollis chuckled. "A roan is a horse with a base color that has white hairs mixed in on their body and neck. Technically, in a blue roan, their predominate color is black, but the white hair can make them look blue-gray."

"She's beautiful, with a temperament to match." The admiration in Lucy's voice warmed Hollis.

Dad had purchased a stallion with the right coloring to breed with one of their mares to reliably get blue roans. Last year's blue roan filly was still on the ranch, and because Hollis had carried on his dad's traditions, they now also had a blue roan foal named Roquefort. As long as their financial situation didn't force drastic measures, horses born at the ranch would stay there until they were four and trained in the basics. Hollis would hang on to some, like Fontina, longer to train them as roping horses.

Will slugged his arm. "Right, Hollis?"

Mind at the ranch, he'd missed whatever his brother had said.

Will wasn't one to miss a beat. "How's tomorrow afternoon sound? Weather's supposed to be nice. It'd be fun to see one of Dad's blue roans in action."

"Ah ..." Neenah shrugged helplessly. "Sure. Maybe she will recognize some of the other horses. Could be fun."

"Great!" Will clapped his hands together. "How about the rest of you?" Yet he focused only on Lucy.

She slid her hands under her thighs, shoulders up by her ears. "Are you sure it should be a group thing? We don't need to—"

"I'll come." Cody's voice was gruff. He and Hollis had been closer in high school, but since Hollis moved back, he and Cody had helped each other with projects around their properties and met for lunch a few times. Never had the guy expressed interest in riding.

"I know my limits." Piper tucked Jasper closer. "I'd better sit this one out."

Graham exhaled his relief and patted his wife's knee. "Horses aren't really my thing either."

"Okay, okay." Will had hardly taken his eyes off Lucy. "How about you? You must know how to ride, being a vet and all."

"The two aren't synonymous, but I did take lessons once upon a time. Just don't put me on a troublemaker."

"Most of our horses are named after cheese. How bad could they be?"

Really? That was how Will thought he could reassure her?

"They were trained by Dad. That's how you know you'll be safe." That, and because Hollis would make sure of it.

"One thirty work for everybody?" Will asked. "We can meet you at the barn. We'll have the horses saddled and ready."

Hollis mentally ran through their horses. As beginners, Cody and Lucy would need obedient mounts who wouldn't spook and scare their riders off horses for the rest of their lives.

"If you're getting the horses ready ahead of time," Lucy said, "then Neenah better get there beforehand with BeeBee."

Cody scowled.

There were dynamics here Hollis didn't understand.

Whatever forces swirled around her in the form of Cody's and Lucy's odd agendas, Neenah's expression stayed clear. "I trailer her relatively often to try different trails around the area, so we're pretty efficient. I'll see you around one fifteen."

Hollis nodded his agreement and kept his smile in place, but his frustration toward his brother simmered. The group dynamics were all complicated enough without Will in the mix.

Chapter Ten

"You're going to be good, girl?" Hollis peered into the soft brown eyes of his mom's horse, Brie.

The creamy white mare nudged Hollis's arm as if to tell him to get going. One of Pepperjack's hooves clopped behind him. Both horses were saddled and ready. It was probably time to stop worrying whether he'd chosen the right mount for Lucy.

As he led the horses into the drive, a truck and trailer rumbled up.

Neenah hopped down from the driver's seat of the big diesel. "Will left you to do all the work?"

"Edam's not in the mood to be caught today." Hollis motioned with his chin toward the pasture where his brother was attempting to collect his horse.

The palomino tossed his head and dodged his owner yet again.

Neenah chuckled and unlatched her trailer. "Just don't put Cody on that one. He looked a little green at the idea of a trail ride."

"Edam's all Will's problem. I'll be right back with Aura."

"BeeBee's mama?"

Hollis nodded. "We'll see if there's anything to horses remembering family."

From inside the trailer, BeeBee whinnied. A horse in the stable called back, but Hollis couldn't be sure it was Aura. At least, not until he had trouble keeping the mare, a blue roan herself, still as he saddled her. She kept fighting to rush ahead as he walked her to the stable yard, and when they came in sight of BeeBee, Aura nearly split his eardrum with another greeting.

By then, Cody stood beside Neenah and a tacked-up BeeBee.

Rather than fight Aura's excitement, Hollis jogged her to BeeBee. The two horses touched their noses together for a long breath. BeeBee tossed her head and nickered, and Aura nickered back.

"That's it?" Cody asked. "The big reunion?"

A rare, soft smile graced Neenah's lips. "I'd say they do remember each other. Maybe Lucy was on to something."

"She knows her stuff." Hollis scanned the drive, but there was no sign of her yet.

Clopping steps behind him marked Will finally leading out a saddled Edam. His brother competed on the palomino at rodeos. Unlike Pepperjack, Edam was high-strung for a trail ride.

Will swung up into the saddle, and Edam danced beneath him.

Cody grimaced at Pepperjack and Brie. "Which one of these beasts is mine?"

"I'm putting you on Aura here. She's as gentle as they come. How much experience have you had?"

Cody pressed his knit cap tighter on his head. "Taking lessons is a rite of passage around here, but nothing since that."

"So back in high school?"

"Middle school, actually."

"All right." Hollis motioned him to follow away from Will and Neenah. As they walked with Aura trailing, he reviewed the basics. At the stable, he outfitted Cody with a helmet and grabbed an extra one for Lucy. On the way back, they stopped at the mounting block.

With one self-conscious glance to see if Will and Neenah were watching—they weren't—Cody used it and was in the saddle in seconds. Hollis kept pace beside Aura on the way back to the others, but Cody didn't need help directing his horse.

Finally, Lucy pulled up in a small, beat-up pickup that must be her personal vehicle. He'd once thought her most suited to princess gowns, but the cowboy hat and boots were growing on him. And on Will, apparently, because he rode over to her and chatted until she reached the group.

Without a glance at Hollis, she grinned up at Cody. "Looking good."

Neenah mounted in one fluid movement. "He's looking tense, is what he's looking." She made a show of shaking out her arms.

Cody's face flared red, but his shoulders inched away from his ears. "I can think of better ways to spend a Sunday afternoon, that's all."

"Yet you volunteered to be here," Neenah teased.

And Hollis had a pretty good guess as to why: Cody had a thing for Neenah. Hollis's choice to put Cody on a horse with a clear affinity for BeeBee would serve the guy well. BeeBee and Aura would naturally gravitate toward each other, keeping their riders equally close.

Lucy stroked Pep's nose. "How's he doing?"

"A lot better with the meds."

"Good. I'm glad you noticed the ulcers early." Lucy ran

her hand down Pep's neck and onto his shoulder, giving the horse space to turn his head, half encircling her from behind. His nose bumped her hat askew, and he breathed on her cheek, blowing hair into her face.

Laughing, Lucy turned and held Pep's face with both hands. "Did I not greet you properly?"

The horse snuffled her winter jacket. Since Pep wasn't going for her pockets, Hollis suspected it was just to say hello and not to scavenge a treat. Seemed the animal was smitten, and Hollis couldn't blame him.

He motioned behind her. "Brie is yours for the day."

Lucy turned and let Brie touch her knuckles with her nose, then Lucy took a slight step back, giving Brie space to get used to her. The greeting suited the horse's personality, and Hollis respected Lucy that much more for noticing and adjusting to the differences between Brie and Pep.

He lifted the helmet. "We ask beginners to wear these."

"Good idea. I'll put my hat in the truck." When she returned and strapped on the helmet, she eyed Brie up and down. "She's a tall one. Do you have a mounting block?"

Cody would probably be happy to hear he wasn't the only one interested in a boost. Hollis motioned across the yard. "It's over there, or I can give you a leg up."

"Okay." She gripped the saddle and mane and lifted her foot so he could support her knee and ankle.

"On three?"

She nodded once. He counted down. She jumped on cue and settled into the saddle with ease. That did not always go that smoothly.

"We make a good team," he said.

She shot a grin down at him.

Will started off, and the others followed—Lucy first, then Neenah and Cody. Hollis took up the rear. He'd rather ride beside Lucy, but at least from back here, he could keep an eye on the less-experienced riders, and he wouldn't have to listen to Will's flirting the whole way.

* * *

The muted shades of the winter landscape added to the peace that blanketed Lucy as she peered at the snow-capped mountains and glowing blue sky. This ride would've been a picturesque memory for the start of Hollis and Neenah's relationship. Except, nothing had started. It seemed Lucy had been right about horses harboring special attachments for a lifetime, because BeeBee and Aura remained side-by-side.

Lucy gathered Cody wasn't very comfortable riding. His horse's dedication to sticking with a well-behaved mount worked out well for him, but it'd help her cause if he were just a little less oblivious to what Lucy was trying to accomplish here.

Equally oblivious, Will rode a short distance in front of her. Unlike her own relaxed mount, his horse seemed ready to break into a gallop at any moment. Hopefully, he could prevent that from happening, because the other horses didn't need any ideas.

She reached forward to pat Brie's neck. "You're a good girl." Maybe if she stockpiled praises, they'd have enough of a bond for Lucy to retain some control in a challenging situation.

"So what would you normally do on a Sunday afternoon if you weren't out on a ride?" Will pulled back on the reins, but he remained ahead.

"I'd be with my own animals."

"Animals? You've got a whole farm or something?"

"Not quite." They came around a bend. The buildings came into view in the distance. The white house looked painted into the landscape by a master's hand. The stable matched the darker hues of the barren trees and the dirt training arena. "I have a bloodhound mix, a few ducks, and a pair of goats."

A swish in the dried grass beside her sounded moments before Hollis's voice. "And two miniature cows."

Will twisted in his saddle, apparently also surprised to find they had company. "Sounds like a farm to me."

"My property's not big enough for the cows, so they live somewhere else. And they're technically not mine."

"We've got to find a way to fix that." Hollis cut a handsome picture against the rugged landscape. Perfectly at ease in the saddle, wearing his hat and canvas jacket, and with stubble on his jaw, he would bring droves of women if he were on the cover of a tourism brochure. And if those ladies heard his steady determination to protect something just because it was important to someone else? He'd be fielding proposals left and right.

Lucy bit her lip at the image but refused to dwell on her jealousy.

She might've read too much into Drake's simple statement the other day. He might only mean to sell off Ovation. Or perhaps he did want to sell Rosie and Jasmine. As long as they went to a good home, she could accept that, couldn't she? Except she had no way to ensure they would go to a caring owner. She was totally at Drake's mercy. And he didn't have much of that to spare. "I'm open to ideas."

"Buy 'em?" Will asked.

"The guy isn't selling," Hollis said.

"We get to rustle some cattle?" Will's voice lifted.

"No." The last thing Lucy needed was to be arrested by her own friends.

"Not sure what other options are out there. Why are the cows important?" Will looked back again.

Lucy bit her lip. Maybe the cows shouldn't be so important.

"Ah." Will chuckled. "They're cute, furry little things?"

She nodded miserably.

"That'll get you every time." Will sucked a breath through his teeth. "You think of offering to go on a date with the guy in return for the cows?"

"Will." Hollis's voice had dropped to a growl.

"I'm not suggesting she do anything *untoward*." He hammed up the word. "I'm just saying, for a date with an intelligent beauty like Lucy here? A guy might reconsider whether or not his livestock's for sale. For example, say you'd go with me to the Ridgeline Grill. I'd consider selling you one of our horses. Not Brie—she's Mom's personal horse—but take your pick from the herd."

"The herd isn't yours to sell, Will."

"Sure it is. A third of it, anyway."

Hollis's jaw ticked.

Lucy interrupted before they could get into it. "I don't have land for two miniature cows. I definitely don't have space for a horse." Or the skill.

"So that's a no on dinner?"

"I'm afraid so. I'm not dating right now."

"Wouldn't have to be anything serious," Will said. "I leave January second. You could get a pricey steak dinner on me."

"You'd probably be horrified by how I like my steak, so no thanks."

This time, Will turned so fully, he rested a hand on the cantle at the back of his saddle. "How do you like your steak?"

She licked her lips. Hollis watched too.

"Well-done?" Will asked in a stage whisper.

She named her favorite dish at Ridgeline Grill, but embarrassment clogged her throat, and it came out in a mumble.

"What?"

She lifted her voice, willing herself to be confident. "I like the steak Alfredo there." The time she'd requested the dish on a date with Drake, he'd changed her order to filet mignon, claiming good steak shouldn't be covered in sauce.

Instead of jumping on that bandwagon, Will shrugged. "I'm a plain and simple ribeye guy myself, but to each their own. If you change your mind, I'll buy you all the steak Alfredo you can eat."

"I'll keep that in mind." Not that she'd ever take him up on the offer.

Still mounted, Will leaned down and opened a gate to allow them all into a pasture that ended at the drive. She guided Brie into the spacious field.

Hollis followed her through the gate, then fell in beside her. "Why did you think your steak order would horrify someone?"

Her mouth went dry. Where Will was carefree and rash, Hollis was loyal and observant. If she didn't want to go spilling her heart to the man, she needed to be more careful about how much she revealed.

"It's got something to do with Drake, doesn't it?"

"He believes no sauce should touch a steak." Though in defense of her order, Ridgeline Grill served the steak atop the noodles with a light drizzle of sauce and seasonings. Alfredo pooled at the bottom of the dish, but very little of it touched the meat unless the diner mixed it together. Which Lucy did.

"Pretty sure there are condiment companies that have made fortunes off people who believe otherwise."

Lucy narrowed her eyes. "How do you order your steak?"

His mouth quirked, and she suspected he liked the same thing as his brother. "You know what steak's purpose is?"

"Nutrition, same as any food?"

He shook his head. "Any old freezer burned hamburger

could do that. Steak is meant to be enjoyed, and no one gets to police how you do that. Promise me you'll—"

"Hey, Holly Boy!" Will's voice came from behind them, underscored by the pounding of hooves. "Race you!" He and Edam flew past.

Lucy jolted as Brie startled then surged forward. The ground blurred, and Lucy bounced wildly. She could hardly breathe. Hardly see. Brie was bolting. She needed to pull back on the reins. But how, without letting go of the horn?

This ride could only end two ways.

One, with Brie deciding to stop on her own.

Two, with Lucy on the ground.

Chapter Eleven

Hollis tamped down his panic and anger. Either emotion would blind him, and he would be no good to Lucy.

In the space of one deep breath, he took inventory of the situation.

Brie's choppy canter would soon toss Lucy. Lucy's high-pitched cries only added confusion. Amazingly, she hadn't dropped the reins. Wasn't using them, though. At least the footing was solid here. They had space. And the land sloped uphill on their left.

Hollis pushed Pepperjack into action. Tie-down horses made a living off launching out of the box from a dead stop. Even retired, Pep answered Hollis's request with a burst of speed.

Hollis remained silent—Pep, and not Brie, might obey a command to stop. As soon as Pepperjack nosed into the lead, Hollis signaled the gelding into a sweeping curve.

Crowded, Brie turned with them and lost steam on the incline.

"Pull back on the reins," Hollis instructed.

Lucy peeled one hand up and complied.

"Whoa." Hollis kept his voice low and projected as much as he could. "Whoa."

The command did, indeed, slow Pepperjack, but combined with Lucy's reining, it also stopped Brie. Thank God. Lucy let out a long, shaky exhale, and her entire back curved as she dipped her head.

"You all right?" His voice came out breathless, more from panic than exertion. If only their relationship were such that he could touch her. Hold her. Feel for himself that she was safe.

She lifted her head and brushed her fingers along her brow, tracing the line of her helmet. Her cheeks puffed up as she exhaled again.

"I've never known her to bolt, but the way Will thundered past—" He clenched his teeth to bite off the complaint. Will and Edam reached the gate at the far end of the pasture. Hollis would save his anger for when he got his brother alone.

Cody and Neenah rode near where Hollis and Lucy had turned off the trail. Hard to tell if they'd had tense moments too, but Neenah lifted her hand in an all-good wave.

"I, um ..." Lucy pushed out another breath. "Wasn't expecting that. This will be the last time you trust a rider who had lessons way back when, huh? Everything I knew flew out the window as soon as she took off."

"I haven't lost trust in anyone but Will." If the urge to deck him had been strong at the brunch, now he was in real danger of losing control. *Lord, help me.*

Lucy's flushed cheeks and shaky smile answered the prayer by pulling his mind back to where it needed to be—with her.

"You stayed on at a canter," he said. "That's a feat for a beginner."

She cringed. "I did dream of being a bronc rider back in the day."

Everything he thought he knew about her dropped away. "You did?"

"Not for a second." Lucy laughed suddenly, as though surprised by her own joke.

Hollis grinned. She hadn't lost her spirit.

"Shall we?" She shifted in the saddle and pointed toward the others.

Below, Cody and Neenah meandered along at a leisurely walk. Will doubled back.

Hollis kept Pepperjack motionless. "Are you still okay with riding? We can get off and walk them home."

"I should be okay as long as she doesn't spook again." She stroked Brie's neck. "But you're not going to do that, right?"

He had to appreciate the bravery. In no hurry to deal with his brother or to share Lucy's company, Hollis pointed Pepperjack toward the gate instead of toward the group. Brie followed along.

"So, was I going a lot slower than it felt like, or did Pepperjack manage some impressive speeds to catch up?"

"I told you the morning we met that he's still got it."

"Little did we know my life would one day depend on that."

Hollis fell silent, mostly because he hated how true it'd been. A helmet could only do so much. If Lucy had fallen, she could've been badly injured.

They rejoined the group near the gate.

Will opened it and waited as Lucy passed through first. "That was quite a run, huh?"

"I would've bailed if I were you," Cody said from behind them.

"That would *not* have ended better," Neenah scoffed. "But herding Brie uphill was good thinking, Hollis."

He dipped his head in acknowledgment as he moved aside and let the others go through the gate ahead of him.

Cody grinned as he rode past. "For a second, I thought you were going to jump on behind her or pull her off onto your horse."

Once through the gate, Hollis lingered to ensure Will secured it behind the group. "Neenah might know more about that kind of stunt than I do. I stuck with what I knew."

"I couldn't have done anything better." Neenah lifted her chin and called ahead to Lucy. "I suppose you didn't see him in action?"

Up on the drive, waiting for the group, Lucy shook her head. "Not really. Was he impressive?"

"Definitely."

Lucy's lips curved in a satisfied smile, but instead of waiting for him to ride beside her back to the stable, she went ahead. Maybe it was his anger at Will or his frustration at not understanding the game Lucy was playing, but suddenly he cared very much that she hadn't thanked him for the rescue.

* * *

Lucy didn't realize she hadn't recovered from her fright until she had all her weight on one foot in the stirrup as she dismounted. Her leg trembled and gave way, and she dropped toward the ground.

"Easy there, Doc." Steady hands braced her waist and eased her descent.

Physically, anyway. Her heart was still falling, hard and fast, for the man who'd caught her.

Feet on solid ground, her hands slid from Brie's saddle, and she turned.

Hollis stood so close, her coat brushed his. He smelled of mountain air, sage, and horses. Or maybe that last one was the animals boxing them in on either side. He studied her intently for one beat, then two, looking like he wanted to say something.

And she ... she wanted him to. Despite her hesitance to date. Despite her vow to avoid feeling small and helpless again, to avoid being at anyone's mercy. Thing was, he'd saved her, both on the ride and just now, yet he hadn't made her feel small either time. Hadn't made a cutting remark or told her she should've known or done better.

If he said the right thing—or, rather, the *wrong* thing?—her heart would be his to do with as he pleased.

Instead, his jaw set, and he took both Brie's and Pepperjack's reins and walked them into the barn. That was good, right? So why did her heart pound like she was once again trapped on a bolting horse?

"How was the ride, kids?" Susan Price approached from the house, two Labrador retrievers at her heels. About halfway across the stable yard, she must've realized not all the horses belonged to the family because she gasped and redirected toward BeeBee and Neenah.

Lucy removed the helmet and smoothed her hair.

Will led Edam and Cody's horse to the stable, and Lucy started after him. "I can help. I still remember how to use a brush."

He waved her off. "I have a feeling Holly Boy has a few choice words for me. For the record, I didn't expect that from Brie."

"It's okay." She swallowed. It *wasn't* okay. Why had she said it was? She tried again. "Everyone survived."

"I'll be sure to tell Hollis you said that." He motioned for the helmet, and she handed it over. "But, just in case, better stay out here where it's safe." He winked and led the horses away.

Lucy stuffed her hands into her pockets and rejoined the others as Susan doted on BeeBee. After untacking the horse and brushing her down, Neenah trailered her, said her good-byes, and drove off. Cody followed suit, but before Lucy could head for her own car, Susan waved her toward the house. "You look like you could use a cup of coffee."

"Oh." Lucy eyed the road out. She could use a warm drink—fading adrenaline left her feeling cold and shaky. But could Susan really see that, or was she interested in talking with Lucy about her intentions with her son?

"It's decaf. Come on in." Susan was already headed for the porch. The dogs raced ahead.

Taking the invitation would give her the chance to finally learn what Susan knew and to correct any assumptions about Lucy's feelings. Also, the brothers were probably arguing right now because of her. Biding her time with Susan might give her the opportunity to smooth over any hard feelings left behind.

* * *

Hollis's anger was primed to snap faster than the quick release rigging they used to train new roping horses. Brie, back to her usual cooperative self, stood in the grooming stall while Pepperjack waited in the breezeway for his turn.

At the sound of hoofbeats, Hollis glanced over his shoulder. Through the bars that made up the top portion of the stall, he spotted Will headed his way with Edam and Aura.

Hollis lifted the saddle off Brie and slung it harder than necessary onto the rack. "That was incredibly reckless."

"None of the other horses bolted." Will secured Edam and Aura then joined Hollis in grooming Brie. "Why did Brie? She have a habit of that?"

Just like Will to find someone else to blame.

"You stormed right past her. What did you think would happen?"

"Nothing. Besides, didn't Dad work on stops from a canter for exactly that reason?"

Hollis clenched his jaw. Dad had trained the family's mounts for a whole list of scenarios, including to stop from various speeds in case of an emergency like the one that had happened on today's ride. "The training doesn't do much good when the rider isn't capable of signaling the horse. Our guest's safety was on us, and you put her in danger."

"Not on purpose. I asked her to dinner. Obviously, I didn't want her hurt."

"If you knew her at all, you wouldn't have done that either."

"Why not?"

"She hasn't recovered from the *last* awful guy she dated."

Will scoffed, and Brie shifted between them.

Okay. Will wasn't as bad as Drake. Dangerously careless, yes, but not calculatingly cruel. They finished with Brie, and Hollis led her out.

"This is about more than Lucy, isn't it?" Will clipped Pepperjack into the cross ties.

Hollis's chest tightened and heated. He clamped his mouth shut before his anger could boil over.

"Look." Will's boot scuffed the floor. "I already feel bad enough about losing all that money."

The guy had lost millions. Literal millions. A couple of uncomfortable emotions didn't set the situation to rights.

Will blundered onward, voice earnest. "I know it put you and Dad in a tough place. I'd pay you back if I could. I just can't. Barely paid my own expenses this year."

Weren't older brothers supposed to be the responsible ones? How could a man ruin his family's stability, then call visiting on holidays the best he could do? Will was a failure, and he just might pull the whole family down with him.

Yet the parable of the unforgiving servant steered Hollis

away from venting the full force of his anger. The Lord required forgiveness. He measured his tone and words carefully. "Then if I were you, I wouldn't claim to own a third of the ranch, because by that logic, you'd be responsible for a third of the debt too."

"You're right." Will cleared his throat. "I shouldn't have said that. In fact, if you want to meet up with a lawyer while I'm home and—"

"No. That's not what I want." Dad had named them and Mom as his joint heirs. He wouldn't want Hollis excluding Will any more than the Lord wanted Hollis demanding repayment for the debt.

"What *do* you want from me?" Will raised his arms as if inviting Hollis to check his pockets for riches. "'Cause the way I see it, I got no way to make you happy. But Dad knew the risks—I explained them to him and to you."

"The difference is, I understood. Dad only knew his son wanted his help. You took advantage. If I hadn't invested, you know Dad would've scrounged up the rest for you from his retirement. You never should've asked for that kind of money from him. The ranch may never recover." As he spoke, his anger swung toward his dad. For gambling everything on Will. For taking a chance building this barn. For getting sick and leaving it all on Hollis's shoulders.

He rubbed his arm, trying to make sense of it. His brother must really have him worked up for him to resent Dad. Sure, the man had taken some risks Hollis wished he hadn't. But he couldn't have known the future.

Hollis pointed his anger back where it belonged—at Will. "As if you haven't done enough damage, you breeze in for Christmas like it's nothing, flirt with Lucy like it's nothing, and come January, you'll leave again like that's nothing too. It's like you're purposely failing to see what's going on here."

Will glared, brow furrowed. "What's going on?"

"That ex of Lucy's? He's burning our reputation. I'm going to have to drop our prices, but this place is already in the red." His voice threatened to crack. "My savings—what's left of them after your stunt—are only going to get us so far. Debts are coming due next summer, and I've only got a tenth of what we need."

Will's mouth worked silently for a moment. "One guy has that much pull?"

"He's connected, and I have no reputation as a trainer. Even without him, this place is something Dad was building. Something unique to his skill set and experience level that I can't duplicate. Not on my own. This is supposed to be a family business, and family is supposed to be here for each other."

Will studied him silently for a few beats, brow creased. "You want me to come back?"

Was that what Hollis wanted? Even if Will sold the RV he called home and moved back into the ranch house, he wouldn't bring any finances with him to supplement what Hollis was already pouring into the business. And yet, Will would be another set of hands.

A set of hands Hollis wanted to trust, despite what had happened with that real estate deal, despite what had happened with Lucy. "You used to look out for me. You saved me from the wrong crowd when I joined the rodeo circuit. You helped me find work in the offseason. You stood by me early on when my mistakes cost us buckles."

Will smirked. "Don't forget, I pulled you out of a pig pen once."

Hollis rolled his eyes. "Sure, that too. And that experience? Just one more example of how I learned to stick with family. Not to wander off on my own. To step in when a family member needs help. I thought you knew those things too. So where have you been? When did you get this reckless?"

Will puffed up his cheeks and blew out the breath slowly. "All your examples, Hollis, are things I did for you. Not for Dad. He and I didn't have the same connection you two did. Maybe you were too young to see it."

No. He didn't get to pull the older brother card when he wasn't acting the part. "I wasn't too young last winter, when he was counting down the days, waiting for you to come home. I think that's why he lasted as long as he did."

"So I could be there to watch him go?" Will's voice strained. "How kind of him to give me those memories."

Hollis's eyes and throat burned. He swallowed hard to check his emotions. "How can you be so selfish?"

Will dipped his head. "I could never do things right for Dad. Even when I came home to say goodbye, first thing he said to me was, 'What took you so long?' He didn't have any deathbed requests for me. Just a deathbed guilt trip."

By coming so late, Will hadn't given him time for much else.

"You could've come home more the whole time he was sick."

"Maybe. Or maybe relationships can be complicated, and I did the best I knew to do."

Hollis shook his head. "And Mom? Was that complicated too?"

Will kept his eyes averted. "I call her once a week. Maybe more. And I always answer when she calls me."

"And now that she and I are the ones trying to figure out how to make this impossible thing work?"

Will licked his lips and scanned as much of the barn as he could see from the inside of the grooming stall. "The way she talks, it's not that bad." Understanding flickered on his brother's face, and finally he met Hollis's eyes. "Because you're keeping her in the dark."

"I'm protecting family. That's why I came back."

"Of course it is," Will muttered. "And Lucy?"

Hollis crossed his arms over his chest. "What about her?"

"You seem to be protecting her too. You have feelings for her?"

Lots of them, but she'd been clear about the limits of their relationship. "She's a friend. One I'd rather not see hurt on our property, on one of our horses. We already have enough bad press."

Will unclipped Pepperjack, now groomed and ready for his stall. "So if Cody's horse had bolted instead, you would've reacted the same way?"

"Yes." Just with less panic.

Will scoffed and led Pepperjack out.

Hollis started on Aura. As he brushed her out, he heard Will approach again. If nothing else, he had to give his brother credit for bravery, hanging around despite knowing how much Hollis blamed him for.

Hollis didn't look up from his work. "We need your help here, Will, but if you're not going to put family first, the least you could do is not sabotage us."

"You never asked for my help."

"I shouldn't have had to." Hollis spared his brother a look over Aura's back.

Anger flashed in Will's face, and Hollis actually found himself hoping Will would argue. Yell. Give Hollis an outlet for all his frustration.

Instead, he turned and walked away.

* * *

In the farmhouse kitchen, Lucy shrugged out of her coat and hung it on a hook by the door. A collection of various chicken figurines roosted atop the upper cabinets. Plants and knickknacks crowded the windowsills. Papers cluttered a desk in the corner, but the countertops themselves were mostly clear. Dinner must've been in the oven, because the savory scent of meat and spices hung in the air.

The dogs trailed Susan as she retrieved two mugs from a glass-paned cabinet, filled them, and brought them to the island. She motioned Lucy toward the sugar packets in a bowl, then retrieved a carton of cream. "I hear you're the one tasked with finding a match for Hollis."

Lucy froze with a now-empty sugar packet suspended over her coffee. She'd figured Susan knew something, but she had never imagined the Carters would be so open about their full mission—or that anyone else would think it a good idea.

Susan perched on a chair at the island. Only as she sat did the dogs give up on following her. One sank onto the cushioned mat by the sink, the other back on the rug at the entry.

"How's it going?" Susan asked.

"Um. Well." She swallowed. Susan didn't seem to be against the idea, and Lucy needed word to get back to the Carters that she was holding up her end of the bargain, lest they resume their own matchmaking. "I had hoped he'd get to know Neenah a little better on today's ride, but ..." She shrugged. "I only promised to make introductions."

"Neenah seems like a nice girl. It sure was nice to see one of Bill's blue roans in good hands." Susan skipped sugar and stirred in a splash of cream. "But I'm not sure she's what Hollis needs."

"Oh. Why?"

Susan wiggled her eyebrows. "If I'm not mistaken, that friend of hers has some real feelings for her."

"Friend of hers? Cody?"

Susan nodded and sipped her coffee.

To buy time, Lucy took a drink too. "They're coworkers. Both police officers. If you saw a bond, that's probably it."

Weren't cops kind of famous for being 'brothers in blue'? By that logic, Cody probably saw Neenah as a sister.

Susan sucked a breath through her teeth. "I could be wrong, but he watches her like Oak and Mable watch me in the kitchen." She motioned to the dogs.

Lucy scratched her temple. "Like he's hoping for something from her?"

"The treat of her attention."

Lucy laughed weakly and closed her hands around her mug. She or Susan had misread the situation, and given the way her matchmaking attempts had fizzled, she suspected herself as the party in the wrong.

One of the dogs barked, and both canines stormed the door. Will kept his head down and passed through to another part of the house.

Ten minutes of small talk later, Hollis entered. He removed his hat and ran a hand through his hair. His sharp blue eyes looked between her and his mom as if he could read a transcript of their conversation on their faces.

Lucy pushed her seat backward and rose. "I'd better get going." She sidestepped Hollis to retrieve her coat. "Thank you for the coffee. And the ride."

Hollis got the door for her, and she jogged down the steps. When she hit the walk, more clunking sounded on the porch. Hollis had followed her out. As he descended the stairs, he crossed his arms. "I had a talk with Will. He understands he was out of line."

"I hope you didn't make him feel too bad."

"For putting you in danger? Of course I did."

The protectiveness in his voice wrapped her up in a sense of security that wouldn't feel more solid if his arms were around her. The thought lit a spark in her belly that sent her heart galloping and stung her cheeks. "Hollis."

He lifted his eyebrows but otherwise didn't budge.

She swiped a hand over her face. "Well, I'm sorry the whole afternoon didn't go differently."

"That's not yours to apologize for."

Only because he didn't know what she'd attempted—and failed—to do. He was supposed to be on his way to the kind of love that would add to his happiness and ease some of the ache of his recent losses. But instead of getting to know Neenah, he'd spent his time looking after Lucy.

Matchmaking was harder than it sounded.

She sighed and stepped back. "Then I guess all I can really say is thank you. I'm glad you were around to make sure Brie's little adventure didn't end badly. I was completely out of my depth, but you knew exactly what to do."

His expression softened, and he dipped his chin. "Anytime."

Such a gentleman. Any single lady ought to be glad for steady, protective company like his. So why hadn't Neenah taken notice of him? Whatever the case, it was probably time to move on to a new introduction.

Chapter Twelve

"**Y**ou're not still working." Lucy feigned shock, though this was exactly what she'd been hoping for when she'd stepped into The Cakery.

Caroline propped her hands on her hips and rolled her shoulders.

Lucy could only imagine how stiff she got, bent over sweets all day as she baked and decorated the delicacies on display. Hopefully, that would make it easier to talk her into a carriage ride. Then Lucy would just have to figure out how to encourage her and Hollis together better than she'd done with Neenah. But, first things first.

She finished paying the cashier for the sugar cookies and four hot drinks she'd ordered and turned a sympathetic smile on Caroline. "Your workday must start early. Don't you deserve some fun too?"

"We had a big order come in today, and someone called in sick, so ..." Caroline shrugged good-naturedly. "You know what they say about when you love your job."

"You never work a day in your life? I love my job too, but

that's completely untrue." Lucy lifted the drink carrier and bag of cookies. "It's carriage ride night. My friends and I all decided at the last minute to enjoy it. You should join us."

Caroline bit her lip and eyed the doorway to the back. "The order's not quite done."

"Then come back after a carriage ride. It'll be a nice break, and what could be more Christmasy? It's even snowing." If the enchanted setting did its thing, perhaps Caroline and Hollis would hit it off so well, he'd offer to come help Caroline finish up.

Although the sweets in the case were exquisitely decorated. Could Hollis maintain that standard? Or maybe Hollis and Caroline working together in the kitchen would turn into a food fight with frosting and cupcake batter and—

Lucy cut off the thought. She was setting Hollis up, but what happened after that? She had no desire to know. She shored up her wobbling smile. "It'll only take an hour, I'm sure."

"You know what?" Caroline pulled the string on her apron. "Why not?"

Two minutes later, Caroline accompanied Lucy out to the bench where her friends waited.

"Caroline, you know Piper and Graham?" Lucy extended the drink carrier to the couple.

"Hi, Caroline." Piper took her tea and passed a hot chocolate to her husband, who had a bundled-up Jasper strapped to his chest.

Lucy set the bag of cookies on the park bench so she could take her chai tea from the carrier and then offered the last member of their party his spiced cider. "And this is Hollis."

Hollis lifted his cup toward Caroline in a greeting before focusing on Lucy. "We know each other. I'm friends with her brother Clint."

Since they lived in a small town, that fact shouldn't surprise Lucy, but she hadn't seen Hollis with Clint recently. She hadn't factored in how that friendship might impact this setup. Still, even if he'd previously only thought of Caroline as Clint's sister, the right circumstances might help him see Caroline in a new light.

Now to arrange said circumstances.

Lucy motioned toward the corner where the carriage rides were departing, and Hollis and Caroline started in that direction without seeming to notice Lucy fall back to walk with Piper and Graham. Between the old-fashioned lampposts, window displays, and strings of Christmas lights, the falling snow glowed, and downtown Redemption Ridge looked fit for a movie. How could a setting like this not inspire a little romance?

Jealousy fell through her core like a broken icicle. She sipped her chai to warm back up.

"I want to know what's going on." Piper had dropped her voice to a whisper, but not a quiet one.

Caroline and Hollis continued chatting ahead of them. Lucy looked past Piper to Graham. Also seemingly oblivious, he rubbed circles that little Jasper probably couldn't even feel on his back through all the layers.

She slowed her step, letting Caroline and Hollis get farther ahead. "Nothing's going on."

Now Graham snorted. He lifted his drink in a none-too-subtle attempt to hide his smirk.

Piper narrowed her eyes. "I've known you for years. You've looked after strays before, but usually they're cute, furry baby animals. This time, your special project is a full-grown and very handsome rodeo star."

Graham grunted. "*Former* rodeo star."

Piper laid a hand on his arm. "Of course. And not nearly

as handsome as you. But you're off the market. Lucy seems to think Hollis isn't, because she keeps pushing single ladies at him." Piper swung her gaze back. "So what's the deal?"

Lucy lifted her shoulder. "Maybe it's like you said. I have a knack for matchmaking."

"Why exercise that knack on Hollis?"

"Dolores and Jack Carter were meddling—telling me things about Hollis and probably ready to give him the inside scoop on me so he'd feel sorry enough for me to go on a few dates—which I didn't want to go on. The only way they'd stop was if I agreed to introduce him around, so here we are. But to my credit, I'm matchmaking minus the meddling."

"I thought meddling was *any* unsolicited interference," Graham said.

Piper's cheeks rounded with a smug smile. "Besides, it kind of sounds like you're setting *yourself* up better than you are anyone else. I hear you were chummy on the trail ride, even before he saved your life."

Caroline and Hollis reached the line awaiting the next horse-drawn carriage and turned to look for them.

Lucy dipped her face. "It's not my fault he and Neenah didn't hit it off. But these two seem to be doing better."

"Are you sure that's what you want?"

"Yes." Lucy washed down the lie with a bite of sugar cookie.

* * *

A two-seater pulled up, and the driver tipped his hat. "All aboard."

Hollis stepped back. Maybe a couple was in line somewhere behind them. "We have a group of five. We can wait—"

"Odds are the next one will be just as small." Lucy

motioned him to climb up. "Our group's going to have to split up."

And that meant he'd get some time alone with Lucy? She didn't have to tell him twice. Hollis took the two steps up into the small rig and turned back to offer her a hand up.

Instead of taking it, she nudged Caroline forward. "I know you have work to do yet tonight, so I'm sure you don't want to wait around forever."

Hollis narrowed his eyes. Was Lucy avoiding him? Or up to something else?

Caroline held her cup near her mouth, like she was using the hot drink to keep her face warm. "Are you sure?"

"Yup." Lucy ushered her to the step like a mom loading a kid on a school bus. "I'm glad you came with us, but I don't want to take up your whole night."

Like the sweet, trusting person she was, Caroline climbed up and settled on the velvety seat without a sideways glance. If only her brother were so trusting, Hollis wouldn't have to worry about what Clint might have to say if word got around about this.

The driver signaled, and the sleek black Standardbred trotted down Redemption Ridge's Main Street. The pace stirred a chilly breeze, so he passed Caroline the blanket wadded up in the corner.

"Lucy must be an includer, huh?" Caroline asked as she arranged the fleece over her lap. "Everyone gets to be part of the fun. Even the local baker she barely knows. That's sweet."

Leave it to Caroline to assume the best.

He noted the streak of flour in her hair. "I take it she roped you into this last minute?"

"Yep." Her smile reached her eyes. "You?"

He nodded. When she'd first called and invited him to meet her, Piper, and Graham, part of him had hoped it was meant to be a double date. Those hopes had been dashed about ten minutes after he'd met up with the group and Lucy had emerged from The Cakery with Caroline in tow.

"She did have a point about me working a lot lately. I haven't gotten out to as much of the usual holiday stuff as I would like." Hands resting on the blanket, she peered at the passing scenery. "Redemption Ridge has always been a special place."

Not all ranching towns had such vibrant downtowns or communities so passionate about pulling together to do things like offer free carriage rides.

Still, he couldn't get sentimental with his best friend's little sister, so he scoffed playfully. "How would you know? You've never tried living anywhere else."

Caroline breathed an indignant laugh. "Believe it or not, I have ventured beyond the town limits. And I meet a lot of people from a lot of places at The Cakery. There's no place like Redemption Ridge."

He sipped his cider. "If you say so."

She eyed him, head tilted. "Are you saying you regret moving back?"

The question sliced through his attempt at levity. "No. Actually, it's the opposite. I wish I hadn't spent so much time away from my folks when I could've just as easily been here every winter."

He could've been training alongside his dad for years, built up a reputation. And how well the added memories of Dad would serve him now. Maybe Will wasn't the only one who'd failed to come through for family.

"What matters is you came home eventually." Her voice softened. "That gives me hope."

Hope for what? Hollis glanced over, but she was staring off, either completely absorbed in the picturesque scene around them or mind elsewhere entirely. Her thoughts were none of his business. He let the conversation lapse, and when she restarted it a block later, small talk carried them through the rest of the ride.

When the carriage stopped, he helped her down. Behind them, a larger carriage advanced with the rest of their party. As it pulled up, Lucy stood quickly, as if that could hide the fact that there'd been plenty of room for two more. If she would've let them wait, they all could've ridden together.

She hopped to the sidewalk, thanked the driver, then beamed at him and Caroline. "Have a good time?"

"Yes!" Caroline squeezed her arm. "Thanks so much for talking me into this, Lucy."

"Of course. The fun doesn't have to end. We were talking about walking around to look at the window displays."

"I do need to get back to that order, but I appreciate the little break."

Lucy's line of sight bounced between him and Caroline. "Should we walk you back to The Cakery?"

Caroline waved her off. "It's nearby, and there are tons of people out tonight. See you around." She bid a quick farewell and set off down the sidewalk.

Lucy frowned after her. "It is dark out. Maybe you should go with her."

Something was definitely up. "Crime is virtually non-existent in Redemption Ridge."

"I wouldn't go *that* far," Graham said.

Fair enough. Hollis had heard some of Cody's stories, and if he thought Clint would have a problem with Hollis taking a romantic carriage ride with Caroline, letting her get mugged would be even worse. "All right." He dipped his head and leaned close to Lucy. "But when I get back, you have some explaining to do."

Her eyes darted to his and the corner of her mouth pinched. Her worry would be adorable if he could relieve it with a kiss, but considering she seemed determined to throw him at any available woman except herself, she wouldn't take kindly to an advance.

He jogged after Caroline, saw her to The Cakery, then met back up with Lucy and the others on the square. They'd wandered just a few businesses down from where he'd left them, but one important thing had changed: They'd added one to their number.

The newcomer was a short woman with a cloud of curly blond hair and a bright red coat. Her horn-rimmed glasses perched on a little nose and seemed to accent the size of her eyes. She motioned excitedly as she spoke to Lucy. "Of course he doesn't want her to help, but how can he say no, right? So then they're, like, working together, and what do you know?" She shimmied her hands.

This was either a gossip session or a retelling of some TV show. Either way, he wanted no part, but Lucy nodded, egging on the story, then lifted her eyebrows as if to ask him, "Interesting, right?"

The woman plowed on. "They actually have way more in common than they thought. It's like an opposites-attract, modern take on *Pride and Prejudice*, and it's perfection." She made the "okay" hand signal with both hands. "I mean, who can resist an opposites-attract romance?" Her voice turned shrill with excitement.

Hollis wanted to raise his hand. Based on the ten seconds of data he'd just gathered, this woman was his opposite, and he could definitely resist. He picked up his pace to pass Lucy and her bubbly friend. Piper and Graham studied the window display one store over, and they'd make much safer company.

"Hollis, do you do any reading?" Lucy's voice halted his progress.

He reluctantly turned back. "The occasional memoir or biography."

The newcomer gasped as she noticed him and clenched a

fist to her chest. Her eyes got as wide as horseshoes. "Hollis Price?" She turned her gaping attention to Lucy. "You know Hollis Price?"

Great. A super fan.

Lucy chuckled. "Hollis, this is Penelope. She works at Bethany's Book Barn. Pen, this is Hollis. Now you know him too."

He touched the brim of his hat and nodded.

Penelope caught his hand on the way back down and clutched it with both of hers. "What an honor. I followed your career since the very start. My dad started taking me to your rodeos all over the state starting when I was, like, eight. He said you were going places. And you did! So amazing. What brings you back to Redemption Ridge?"

He hadn't expected the rapid fire of her praise to end on that down note. Grief kicked him in the chest, and he pulled his hand away. He barely managed a smile. "Family."

"That's so great." She launched down that line of thought, the Thoroughbred of talkers.

He moved aside to put Lucy between them as they started after Graham and Piper, but Lucy slipped by.

Penelope's arms flailed, and she latched onto Hollis. "Whoops. The snow makes it slick."

She'd have been fine if she'd worn sensible shoes, but Hollis bit his tongue.

Penelope squeezed his bicep. "Lucky for me you were right here, huh? To think, I almost didn't even come tonight, but then I would've missed all this." She waved a hand at the twinkling street so enthusiastically, she tipped against Hollis again. Giggling, she straightened, but she kept her hand in the crook of his arm.

He decided against shrugging her off because she probably would fall without the support. He didn't know why Lucy was throwing him to the wolves—or Little Red Riding Hood, perhaps, considering Penelope's coat—but this just confirmed again that something had changed since the first morning they'd met.

Back then, she'd rescued him from her over-eager assistant, but now if Pen *did* wipe out, he had a feeling Lucy would be right there, insisting he carry her all the way to a hospital.

Chapter Thirteen

Were Rosie and Jasmine bulking up? Since Drake had purchased them as adults, their size ought to remain steady. She ventured across the dry winter grass to their trough but saw nothing unusual. Maybe it was all in her head, planted by what Drake had said last week about charity cases.

The sun had set before five, and though the sky turned inky, flood lights on the barn washed the pastures in light that even spilled onto Ovation standing at the fence. Dark ground covered the area. Mud? She looked over her shoulder, but Drake had left the gate. If he was in the barn, she might be able to make it out to Ovation's pasture and back before he realized she'd taken a field trip.

The cows followed her to the back of their paddock, and there Lucy again checked for Drake. Good thing he had so many lights on his house, assuring her he didn't lurk in any shadows on the porch. She let herself through the back gate and jogged across the empty paddock between the two enclosures.

Ovation tossed his head as she neared. The deepening

twilight dulled his beautiful coloring, but even the receding light couldn't hide the mud splotching his legs. From the looks of it, he'd paced the fence until he'd worn away the grass, then spent most of his time standing in the muck he'd created.

"That's not good for you, sweetie." She held the back of her hand out.

The horse sniffed her direction, stomped, and took off to the far side of his paddock. He had a lean-to shelter, water, and hay, but no company here. Unless there were other horses in surrounding pastures, out of sight because of the hilly landscape?

Although that raised the question of what might be out of sight in the pasture where she stood. Aside from the day she'd found Rosie and Jasmine here, she'd never seen anything in this one, but cow droppings suggested something was. Just her luck, it'd be an ornery bull.

Ovation's head lifted, and he shifted like he'd spotted a threat. She probably should leave the poor creature in peace. Besides, the cookie decorating competition at church started soon. She turned, watching her feet to avoid stepping in manure.

Instead, a pair of boots came into her field of vision. "Something of interest out here?"

Her muscles tensed like they had when Brie bolted. She'd frozen up then, but she couldn't afford to do that now. Not without Hollis nearby to save her. She prayed the Lord would give her the right approach to deal with this situation. That spirit of power.

Maybe she ought to fake it until she made it. God cared about all his creatures, Ovation and her cows included. Surely, He would help her defend them. She pulled her shoulders back, lifted her chin, and resumed her course for Rosie and Jasmine's enclosure. "That mud isn't good for him."

"The mud's worse than usual. Last night's snow melted. Not much I can do about that." Drake's voice and footsteps came from behind her right elbow, but he quickly gained on her. "But now you know why I asked you to check him for thrush."

Her surprise almost had her sputtering defenses, but a calm not her own prompted her to wait the space of a breath. Thrush was a bacterial infection that could fester in moist conditions. Treatment was easy enough if dealt with early—clean the hooves, apply iodine, and keep the horse out of ongoing excessive moisture. "I don't remember that conversation."

"You were here to see the cows."

Said cows mooed at her as she worked on the gate that would allow her into their paddock. "You're going to have to be more specific. I come twice a week for that."

"It was the time I asked you to check Ovation's hooves." Disdain and frustration powered his tone.

This was spiraling. The truth was supposed to set her free, so she clung to it. "You've never asked me before." If he had, she likely would've acted immediately. Drake ought to have everything necessary in the barn.

He exhaled long and slow. "I can't help it if you have a bad memory, but don't apologize to me. The horse is the one paying the price. Although he's pretty content to act like a wild horse, so he can't complain."

Her anger brandished rash responses, but she knew better than to try to argue or reason with him. She focused instead on securing the gate behind herself and Drake so Rosie and Jasmine wouldn't take another field trip. "If I didn't have other plans to get to, I would do it now. As it is, it'll have to wait until Saturday." She dusted her hands as she turned from the fence. "Ten a.m. work?"

"I'm running a petting zoo for you." He lifted his hands

away from Jasmine's curious nose. "The least you could do is be flexible."

The cows fell in line as she headed for the exit. "When would you prefer?"

"I'm out of town on business this weekend. The next time you can come out is Tuesday at six."

Tuesday, two days before Christmas. She was technically free, but she usually visited at least once over the weekend. "You must have someone coming to care for the animals while you're gone. I can come at the same time as them."

"I don't see why my cousin should have to deal with you."

They stepped into the drive, and she again ensured the gate latched. "Because you wouldn't want a horse to go lame from neglect."

His eyes flashed, but he was playing a dangerous game, giving Ovation the bare minimum of care and treating him in such a way that the horse feared him. If he crossed the line into blatant abuse, they could make a case against him.

"What time is your cousin coming on Saturday?" she pressed.

Drake's jaw pulsed. "I'll ask, but I'm not going to make him arrange his schedule around you."

"No problem. I'll be here when he is." She escaped to her truck. As she drove away, she replayed the conversation. In the past, she'd often doubted her own sanity in the face of his lies. At least this time, she'd resisted debating facts. And she'd gotten her way—she could see to Ovation's hooves over the weekend. She thanked the Lord for those victories.

Still, her insides squirmed with tension. She hated face-offs with Drake. Hated the reminder that she'd once trusted him, enjoyed his company, and been flattered by his attention—all feelings she now had for Hollis. If she'd been wrong once, she could be wrong again.

* * *

Lucy pulled her focus from the table across the room to see what had inspired Piper's giggle fit.

Her friend set down a reindeer-shaped cookie with polka-dot antlers and one eye that was four times the size of the other. "There's no way we're winning this thing."

"What ..." Lucy bit her lip. She didn't even know how to ask what Piper had intended without sounding insulting.

Piper's giggles renewed. "The antlers were supposed to look like they had Christmas lights strung on them, but instead they look like ... they're made of gumballs."

"And the eye?"

"I was thinking of a cute puppy with a spot around his eye, only the reindeer version. I just ..." She snorted. "I guess using black for both the eye and the spot was my downfall."

Lucy nodded slowly. Indeed, the choice hadn't helped.

"But what matters is we had fun, right?" Piper elbowed her. "Look at Graham and Grandma. *They* are taking this way too seriously to have fun."

Graham was an excellent cook, known to bake on occasion. His decorating skills might not be top-notch, but apparently Piper's grandma had trusted him enough to team up with him for tonight's event. Nearby sat Piper's grandpa, holding baby Jasper while sharing a plate of sweets with Bryce.

Cody and Neenah also occupied a spectator table, snacking and visiting with friends from the community. The last member of their regular group, Hollis, worked with Caroline at a decorating station across the room.

Every time Lucy glanced over there, her stomach churned. When did he and Caroline get so chummy? He'd acted stiff with her the night of the carriage ride.

Piper tipped her head so close, Lucy could smell her shampoo. "I don't know how Hollis talked Caroline into being his partner for this, but honestly, I'm not sure anyone stands a chance against her. I mean, you've been in The Cakery. You've seen her work."

"Hollis might prove to be a handicap," Lucy said.

"Maybe. I mean, the man's practically a superhero on a horse. He must have some fatal flaw. It could be an inability to handle a frosting bag." Piper bent close to her next cookie. "Or perhaps it's an inability to focus on the work because the competition is too interesting."

Hollis's eyes were definitely not on the competition. He hadn't glanced Lucy's way once all night. Instead, he and Caroline talked and laughed as they decorated one cookie after the other.

"*You*, Lucy." Piper pushed an unfrosted cookie toward her. "I'm talking about you."

"Oh." Feeling foolish, Lucy lowered herself into one of the chairs behind the table and picked up a brown icing bag to put the base on the next reindeer.

"Why are you so bothered by them? I thought you were setting Hollis up with her."

Lucy groaned. Why did Piper have to see right through her? "I'm happy for them. I just didn't realize they'd made plans until they walked in together."

"You're staring at them because they surprised you?"

Doors had opened on the church an hour ago as people started arriving for the annual cookie decorating competition. By now, Lucy should've adjusted to the sight of Hollis with Caroline. Smirking, he slid Caroline a cookie, and whatever he'd done to it made her burst out laughing. Meanwhile, opposing emotions built in Lucy.

"I'm thinking it's more like jealousy," Piper said.

Lucy clenched her jaw. She couldn't deny it, but she also

couldn't indulge feelings like that. "I talked to Drake today. I can't believe I once fell for *him*."

Piper's bag of frosting dipped as she tilted her head. "How's that related?"

"If I got it wrong once, I might again. No, thank you."

Piper pursed her lips and lifted her brows. "So you figured you'd take the sweetest person in Redemption Ridge and set her up with a guy you're not sure is trustworthy?"

Lucy bit her lip. That was a good point. She was no better than Drake, sending someone out to check the hooves of a supposedly dangerous horse.

Piper's tone softened. "You do see the ways Hollis is different from Drake, right?"

Since her breakup, she'd learned more about how narcissists worked. Drake wasn't as bad as they came, but he did display the traits. Love bombing at first, then eventually complaining about time she spent on her friends instead of him. Criticizing her but acting like he was doing her a favor. The constant lies. Making her doubt her own sanity.

Hollis had never been anything but honest. Kind. He'd joined her friends instead of trying to separate her from them. He'd never attempted to control or demean her. Being near Hollis was like cozying up beside a living room fireplace, all safety and warmth. Unless she got too close and the heat of attraction threatened to engulf her better sense. Only friendship was safe. As long as he was just a friend, he wouldn't have nearly so much power to turn her heart to ash.

"Well." Lucy finished the reindeer with a flourish. "If he's so different, I don't have to worry about setting him up with one of the sweetest people in Redemption Ridge, do I?"

Piper pinned her with a stern look. "Except you have feelings for him, and you deserve happiness too."

"So does Caroline. And look at them." She motioned with

the cookie, then passed it to Piper to add the details. "They look happy."

So happy she wanted to go find a corner for a good cry. She averted her gaze.

Piper sighed and went to work on the reindeer. "They certainly do. But you can't live your whole life distrusting men because of Drake. If you're going to pick one man to take a chance on, my vote is for Hollis. Preferably *before* you convince him someone else is a good idea."

If she could convince him to love someone else, she didn't want him in her life, anyway. Maybe setting him up was another way of protecting herself, another test of his character. One he was failing miserably by falling for Caroline.

"Drake was very different," Piper said. "He started nice, but he was too nice, you know? He was shifty if you asked about the wrong things, and he never introduced you to his people. I'm not sure he has any. Hollis *does* have strong connections. He's forthcoming and sincere."

Lucy ran her palms over the thighs of her jeans. Maybe so, but ... "I can't believe I didn't see through Drake sooner. The signs were there. I just didn't know what they meant. Or, I knew but couldn't believe someone would behave that way."

"Exactly. Because you never would. That's a positive about you. You did the best you could with the information you had, and now you have more information. I think you should be proud of yourself for seeing it when you did. Instead of holding a bad experience against yourself, use it as an advantage to help you choose better next time."

"What if I can't, though? People repeat their mistakes all the time."

"Then God will be with you in that too—which actually sounds a lot like the advice you gave me once upon a time, doesn't it?"

Lucy swallowed hard. She much preferred giving advice to getting it.

"Speaking of God, have you prayed about whether you're doing the right thing with Hollis?"

Guilt poked her like a burr. She hadn't. Asking the Lord for power and truth during her last conversation with Drake had resulted in an outcome she couldn't have achieved herself. Would God have changed the course of her interactions with Hollis if she'd consulted Him? She stole another look across the room.

Caroline reached for a bowl, but Hollis blocked her and hogged it for himself. She threw her hands up and muttered something before going back to work without it. The glare she shot him, though, seemed to barely cover a smile.

"Five minutes!" The time call came from a sweet older lady who hadn't looked like she'd had it in her to bellow like that.

A stack of undecorated cookies waited in front of Lucy and Piper.

Lucy brushed her hair off her forehead with the back of her wrist. "You're right. We're never going to win this thing."

"Promise to think—and pray—about what I said?" Piper watched Lucy instead of getting to work on the last cookies.

"Yes, all right?" Lucy pushed the plate closer to her friend.

Piper picked up another sugar cookie and smeared on frosting. "Then tonight's a win in my book."

She took in Hollis and Caroline, heads bent together, one more time. A win, maybe, but not for her.

* * *

"Price." The curt voice cut the December air.

Frozen pebbles ground against the asphalt as Hollis turned beside his pickup in the church parking lot. He let out a half-laugh of relief when he realized the speaker had been Clint. He mimicked his friend's gruff tone. "Taylor."

Clint checked both ways before crossing the lane to reach him, but his furtive movements better fit checking for witnesses than traffic. He crossed his arms tightly as he approached. "My sister? Really?"

Hollis lifted his hands. He'd asked Caroline to warn her brother, but apparently she hadn't. Or, if she had, Clint hadn't accepted what she'd said and wanted to hear it from Hollis himself. "We partnered up for a friendly competition. Nothing more."

"She's a little young for you, don't you think?"

Hollis's mouth dropped open. He knew Clint was protective over Caroline, but he'd expected his friend to believe his first denial. He had nothing to be ashamed of, and Clint should know it. Perhaps he did and the angry-brother act was a prank.

Two could play that game. "You calling me old?"

"You've got about a decade on her. When you were graduating high school, she was in *second grade*."

"Way to make that weird." Hollis rubbed his eyes with the heels of his palms. "You can relax. Like I said, we paired up as friends for the competition. Nothing more."

Clint's eyes narrowed. "Why her?"

"Did *you* want to be my partner? Didn't figure you'd want to leave Nora's side."

"Do you see Nora now?" Clint lifted his hands.

"Yep." Hollis pointed toward Clint's parked vehicle as Nora slipped into the passenger seat.

Clint grunted, and his lips thinned into a line. "Why Caroline?"

"I don't know if you've noticed, but she's made a name for herself in baked goods, and this *was* a cookie competition."

Clint's jaw ticked.

"Fine. Lucy's been trying to set me up with any female she can shove my way."

Clint's eyebrows drew ever lower.

Might as well be totally honest. "I told Caroline exactly what Lucy's been up to. Asked her to spare me another awkward setup. She took pity on me and agreed."

"So to avoid a date with someone else, you figured you'd date *my sister*."

"It wasn't a date. It was about *avoiding* a date. Caroline might as well be my sister too, for how I feel about her."

Clint's steely glare demanded he fill in even more of the story.

Hollis dusted his hand against his pant leg. How Clint knew to push this so hard, he'd never know. The guy must be a lot more observant than he let on. That, or Hollis wasn't any more subtle at hiding an alternative agenda than Lucy was. "I also hoped to test how Lucy would feel if she succeeded in pairing me up with someone."

"And you put my sister in the middle of it?"

Caroline was an adult, but something told him pointing that out wouldn't get him very far. "I was very clear with Caroline what Lucy was up to, and that I wasn't interested in more than casual friendship."

"So now my sister's not good enough for you?"

Hollis cocked his head and opened his mouth, but he was too confused to speak.

Clint lifted his eyebrows, a silent prompt for an answer.

"Caroline's nice, but I'm ..." Could he say it? He was interested in Lucy?

A guffaw broke through Clint's serious expression, and he slugged Hollis's shoulder. "Lighten up, man. I'm messing with you. I *definitely* don't want you to like my sister."

Hollis managed the requisite smile and nod, but he couldn't breathe. Realization hit harder than the ground did after a fall off a horse. He wasn't interested in Caroline or any of the other women Lucy had foisted on him because of his feelings for Lucy herself.

On one level, he'd recognized an attachment to her, but he'd been content to pass it off like a game, since that was how Lucy had been treating him. Only now, as he considered how little appeal anyone else held for him, did he realize the depth of his feelings. If the tables had been turned and it'd been Lucy with another man, he would've put Clint's protective streak to absolute shame. If this was a game, it was a version of Capture the Flag, only with hearts. She already had his and didn't even know it. He either needed to steal it back or capture hers in return. Neither mission would be easy.

Clint's hand landed back on his shoulder. "The part I'm serious about?"

Hollis lifted his gaze. Clint was one surprise after another tonight, and something told Hollis his friend only pulled out this serious tone when he had something vital to say.

"You want to know how Lucy feels about something? Don't put anyone else in the middle of the drama. Man up and ask her."

Hollis's stomach turned to ice. Lucy had been clear where she stood on dating, and she'd given him no indication she'd changed her mind. Quite the opposite, really. "Understood."

"Smart man." With a wave, Clint set off for his own vehicle.

People trickled from the church, among them a familiar silhouette, graceful and tall. He liked Lucy for her kind heart, her compassion for the animals in her care, and her obvious head for business. He even liked her for her concern for him—though he'd rather she'd funneled it in a different direction. But that, too, he understood.

Drake had hurt her. Continued to hurt her.

To capture her heart, he needed to prove himself trustworthy. No more games. No mistakes. Since there was no way he'd be able to drag his own heart back, he couldn't afford for her to lock up her affections any tighter than she already had.

She spotted him and waved.

As Hollis waved back, he prayed the Lord would free her from the pain Drake caused and that He'd use Hollis to help.

Chapter Fourteen

ucy might've failed to pray leading up to her interactions with Hollis, but she'd sure doused today's mission in requests to the Almighty. She collected her tools, the iodine solution for treating thrush, and a couple of old towels and hopped from the cab of her truck.

A man rounded Drake's barn. He spat onto the pavement and ambled up. "Here to see to the wild one?"

She prayed that wasn't a fair description of Ovation. She was no trainer, but she'd worked with challenging horses in her veterinary practice. Between that experience and the extra reading she'd done to prepare for today's visit, hopefully she could manage to clean and treat his hooves.

Still, a scared animal could be unpredictable, and a bite or kick could do real damage. Maybe it was good that Drake had ensured she wouldn't be here alone. This way, someone could call for an ambulance if needed. "You're Drake's cousin?"

He nodded once and motioned her to follow into the barn. For a moment, she thought he'd already collected Ovation from the field. He dashed that hope when he took a

136

halter and lead from a hook and continued out the back of the barn toward where Ovation waited in the mud.

Drake had been wrong: The ground remained just as soggy as a few days before. She could lead him to a dry spot, but the muck already coating him would make his hooves slippery and hard to see. Not to mention, she'd be covered in manure-laced goop by the time she left, and Ovation would quickly repack his hooves with bacteria-growing mud.

"He needs to get out of this pasture at least long enough for his hooves to dry out—regularly."

Her escort shrugged. "You catch him, you can lead him wherever you want."

"Is there an open stall for him?"

"Sure, knock yourself out."

She swallowed hard. Given the situation, she was in danger of doing just that. As they approached the fence, she prayed for help tamping down her fear and low expectations. Horses tuned in to the moods of the people handling them. If Ovation fed off her fear, he might fulfill each of her awful imaginings. She needed that spirit of power—or at least confidence—and hopefully, for the horse's sake, the Lord would grant it to her.

Ovation held his head high with his ears perked toward their advance.

Lucy's arm hit something. Drake's cousin had stopped walking and extended the halter toward her. She juggled her supplies to take it from him. Normally, her job didn't include catching and haltering her patients, but this gruff caretaker wouldn't set a good tone for the interaction anyway. She was better off working on her own.

Rosie or Jasmine lowed behind her in their pasture by the barn. She resisted turning to look. A visit with her cows would be her reward once she finished up here.

Drake's cousin remained about ten feet back. Ovation's

black tail swished as she let herself into the pasture. She set down everything but the halter and lead. "Hey there, sweetheart. I'm here to see about your feet. Are they hurting?"

Her tone didn't have the soothing effect she'd hoped for. Ovation cantered away.

Lucy took a long inhale of the cool mountain air. There were worse things to be doing than earning a horse's trust in a pasture with beautiful mountain views, especially when she understood where the horse was coming from because of her own experience with Drake. When she finished, she'd enjoy telling Hollis she'd helped Ovation in some way.

The horse paced at the far fence.

Following the advice she'd read about catching difficult horses, she stayed in Ovation's line of sight and meandered in his general direction, using a less direct approach than the one that caused him to bolt moments before.

"I'm not a trainer." A human would never hear her quiet words over the distance that separated her from Ovation, but horses had better ears. Hopefully, her tone of voice would convey her good intentions. "You'd be better off with Hollis, I'm sure. But I'm the only one Drake will let close to you, so I'll have to do."

The gelding took a step toward her, and she stopped her trek on the chance the horse would come to her.

Instead, Ovation trotted off again, and Lucy resumed her roundabout stroll toward him. "I know what happened to you. Or I have an idea, anyway. Drake mistreated you, and now you don't trust anyone." Unexpected tears pricked her eyes.

Ovation tossed his head and moved to the side, but not farther away.

Lucy swallowed the lump in her throat. "My friend says I should only write off Drake, not all men. But I get it. Once one person hurts you, it's hard to believe another will treat you better, isn't it?"

Ovation loped along the fence and through the mud he'd created with his constant pacing.

Frustration and grief stung her eyes, and a tear dropped to her cheek. She'd come to help, but Ovation didn't trust her. How like him was she? She'd run from any idea of Hollis as more than a friend. But there was a difference here. Hollis hadn't minded the distance she'd maintained; he'd gone and cozied up to someone else. But Lucy wasn't going to give up on Ovation.

Her phone rang, but she let it go to voicemail, blinked her eyes clear, and resumed her strategy. In the article she'd read, the trainer caught the horse in under fifteen minutes.

Ovation didn't close the distance between them until thirty minutes later. Lucy moved beside him, hoping to halter him. His black mane was tangled, and his beautiful gray coat needed a thorough brushing. The black markings on his legs were splotched with mud as high as his knees.

"That's not good for you, buddy. If you're cooperative, I'll get some brushes, and we'll work on all of it, not just your feet." She spoke smooth and low.

He jerked his head, escaping the first attempt to put the halter on. She tried again. He lifted his nose as high as it reached. The halter and lead, partially on, yanked from her fingers. His big, muscled body shoved her aside. She tumbled back, hit the ground. Pain shot through her wrist.

Thundering hoofbeats faded as Ovation reached the end of the pasture.

Lucy cradled her wrist, the throb already dulling. Not a serious injury, then, thank God.

The halter lay in the yellowed grass fifteen feet away. The gelding stood sentinel by the fence, his dark mane stirred by a breeze, distant evergreens and snow-capped peaks framing him. Her jeans turned damp and cold. Holding her wrist to her chest, she pushed up onto her shaky legs. That could've been a lot worse.

She moved her injured hand one way and then the other. Her tendons burned like she'd poured too-hot tap water over them, but they didn't refuse. The joint did, however, feel warm. She ought to ice it sooner than later, and this job had been challenging enough before she'd been hurt and shaken up.

Ovation's ears pointed in her direction. He'd wanted to get away, not to hurt her. Maybe she hadn't followed the process well enough. Maybe she hadn't been calm enough.

Even if she could catch him now, she couldn't safely clean and treat his hooves. He needed a horse trainer with experience and instincts. The sense of failure hit as sudden and sharp as the pain in her wrist. She hated to leave any creature to deal with the fallout of Drake's mistreatment alone. "We'll figure something out."

His ears twitched, but he didn't step away from the fence, as if he could tell the vow was empty. After all, how many times had she made similar promises to Rosie and Jasmine?

Lucy laid the towels over her forearm and carried the rest of her things in her uninjured right hand back to the gate. Drake's cousin had wandered off sometime during the half an hour she'd spent trying to establish trust with Ovation.

She retraced her steps through the barn and dropped off her tools at the truck before letting herself into Rosie and Jasmine's paddock. The cows munched by the trough as Drake's cousin carried a now empty bag away.

Their usual supplement came in a green package, but whatever he'd poured out for them came from a bright yellow bag. One with an illustration of corn on the front.

"That's the wrong feed for these two." Lucy cut across the field. "In winter, they get hay and cubes, not corn."

He side-stepped a pile of manure. "Take it up with Drake."

"He and I have already discussed their feed." Corn fattened beef cattle for slaughter. Since Rosie and Jasmine were pets, she'd advised a diet of grass, hay, and supplements. "This isn't it."

"He told me it was."

"How long has he been feeding them corn?"

"He'll be back in a few days. You can ask him all the particulars." He stomped away.

The cows gobbled up the corn. Maybe she'd been right when she'd noticed the cows seemed bulkier. If Drake had been feeding them corn for any length of time, he must've been careful to hide it from Lucy. She'd never seen corn scattered around by their feeder before.

Her stomach rolled. How had she failed to expect the worst of Drake?

Lord, I need to be free of him. All of us do.

Her phone sounded, and she automatically reached for the device with her left hand. Her wrist complained with a snap of pain, another injury she blamed on no one but Drake.

She reached into her far pocket with her good hand and answered.

"Can you fit in a stop at Price Quarter Horses?" Chantal asked. "They have a colicking horse."

This day was one piece of bad news after another.

Unless this was simply Jack and Dolores losing patience. "Who did the call come from?"

"Hollis. You want me to meet you there?"

Hearing his name brought a sense of well-being. Except that if he'd called himself, this was an actual concern and not another ploy by their would-be matchmakers. His must've been the call she'd missed while out with Ovation. She'd forgotten to check for a message when she'd called it quits.

She started for her truck. "How soon could you get there?"

"Ten minutes." From the rustling sounds, Chantal was already in motion.

"It'll take me about twenty. See you there." Lucy disconnected.

Even with a twisted wrist, she could handle a colic exam alone. What she couldn't confidently do was handle Hollis. The night of the carriage rides, he'd sounded frustrated at best when he said he wanted to talk to her. He'd caught on to her matchmaking, or at the very least had questions about the admittedly sloppy way she'd sent him off with Caroline. But since he'd ended up bonding with the woman, his anger might've faded. Trouble was, she also didn't want him thanking her for her efforts. She wanted to forget all about the couple. She pressed her good hand to the new ache in her stomach.

Painful stomachs were the key here—she needed to get going to see to the sick horse. With that on his mind, Hollis might not bring up his love life at all. Especially not with Chantal there.

At her truck, she fished out an instant ice pack and squished it around to activate the cooling effect. She drove with it balanced over her wrist.

Twenty minutes later, she approached the turn for Price Quarter Horses. The pasture where Brie had bolted with her lay to the side. The slope of the land shaded patches of snow from the shining sun.

Maybe part of her ought to feel anxious, thinking about Brie bolting. Feeling helpless was one of her most hated experiences. But instead, she felt ... reassured. She hadn't been through it alone. Hadn't had to take care of everything herself.

Hopefully, she could be a similar presence to Hollis today.

Chantal's sedan was already by the stable, but there was no sign of her or Hollis. Lucy set aside the ice pack, collected her kit, and listened for voices. Hearing nothing, she headed into the open stable.

Someone she hadn't seen on the property before was putting a horse in a stall. A boarding client, maybe. Hollis and Chantal might be either direction. She was about to set down her kit so she could use her good hand to text Hollis when jogging footsteps advanced from behind her.

"Thanks for coming." Hollis's voice was a familiar comfort, like a favorite song on the radio. "Allow me." His hand brushed hers on the handle of the kit.

Normally, she liked to carry her own equipment. It was a subtle way of proving she could hold her own in a physically demanding profession, but the tingles racing up her fingers to her arm opened her hand, and Hollis got his way.

"Which horse is it? One I've met?"

He pointed ahead. "Pepperjack."

"Oh no." She pushed the pace and reached the stall first.

Pepperjack's dusty white head appeared in the opening in the door, and he nickered softly. A sweet greeting for a sick horse.

Hollis rolled the door open. "He hasn't been eating."

She retrieved her stethoscope from her kit, careful not to use her injured wrist. If Hollis noticed she'd been hurt, he'd want to know how, and with Pepperjack's health on the line, this wasn't the time to talk about Ovation.

Pepperjack extended his nose toward the brim of her hat, but Lucy dodged his attempt to knock it off and held the stethoscope to his side. "Any other symptoms?"

"Curling his lip, nipping at his side."

"His heart rate isn't elevated, so that's good." She moved the stethoscope to Pepperjack's belly. As she listened for signs of digestion, her gaze wandered to the feeder. Odd that an experienced horseman like Hollis had left hay available to a horse he thought had a digestive problem. "Either silence or unusually loud noises would be red flags, but I'm hearing the normal gurgles." She looped the stethoscope behind her neck and studied the horse.

He wasn't sweating and showed no signs that he'd been rolling. The hallmarks of discomfort Hollis had mentioned were also absent. Pepperjack appeared alert and curious, not dulled by pain.

Still, Hollis knew horses, and he wouldn't call her out unless he was concerned.

She checked Pepperjack's gums. The task took both hands, and she winced at the heat in her wrist. Thankfully, Hollis remained behind her, somewhere near the door of the stall. She forced her eyes to focus. Pepperjack had normal capillary refill.

As far as she could tell, this horse was healthy.

And the supply of hay might mean Hollis knew it as well as she did.

And if he knew Pepperjack was healthy, he'd called her out here to corner her over something else.

"Where's Chantal?" she asked.

"Will had a question about Edam."

Sure he had. Lucy stepped back from Pepperjack. The next step in a colic exam was to pull on a shoulder-high glove and check the internal organs through a rectal exam. It hardly seemed fair to subject a healthy horse—or herself—to that unnecessarily. Unfortunately, the alternative was to face the cowboy behind her. She let out a long breath and turned.

Hollis leaned against the doorframe, arms crossed, one ankle crossed over the foot that held his weight. His dark hat

—his nice one, not the older tan one he usually wore around the ranch—contrasted with the light blue of his eyes. He lifted his eyebrows. "Need me to find a glove in your kit?"

"Are you going to let this get that far?"

His mouth pulled into a smile as slow and sure as a sunrise, and her stomach swooped. "Doesn't seem any more unpleasant than what you've been doing to me."

She cleared her throat. "Your poor horse."

"Pep's pulled his share of pranks over the years."

As if to prove it, Lucy's hat tumbled forward, propelled by what could only be Pepperjack's nose behind her.

Hollis caught the hat but didn't offer it to her. "What exactly *have* you been doing to me?"

Lucy bit her lip and eyed the hat. If he wouldn't let her leave, the least he could do was offer her some cover. "What do you mean?"

"Do you always bring Chantal on calls like this?" He cocked his head. "Or are you throwing her at me next?"

"I haven't thrown anyone at you." Nudged, maybe. Arranged. Not *thrown*.

"I wrote off the stuff with Neenah, but a horse reunion? Really?"

She stabbed her fists onto her hips, not realizing her mistake until pain cut through her wrist. A startled breath wheezed through her lips.

Hollis's teasing expression eased into one of concern. Without taking his eyes off her, he set her hat on her kit.

She lifted her chin. "The horses did recognize each other. I can't help it if you didn't think it was sweet."

His scrutiny continued.

She was about to fess up to the mild sprain when Pepperjack's nose popped into her peripheral vision and he exhaled, moist and loud, into her ear. Muffling a cry of surprise, she ducked away. As she straightened, she found herself inches from Hollis.

The corners of his lips lifted, and his gaze slid from his horse back to her, almost as though to silently thank the brute for smoking her out. She was surrounded, on one side by a horse who'd love her to death, on the other by a cowboy she couldn't possibly indulge her feelings for.

She understood Ovation better and better. If she thought it would work, she might try to charge her way out of this situation. As it was, she'd probably just bounce off him and wind up hurting her other wrist too.

"What's your excuse for arranging a carriage ride for me and Caroline? She was as unsuspecting a victim as I was."

"Don't say that like I committed a crime."

"You're lucky Clint didn't press charges. And you want to argue that setting me up for a romantic downtown stroll with Penelope wasn't a crime?"

Penelope had been a pretty desperate move on her part. She stifled the urge to apologize. "If you found it romantic, it couldn't have been that bad."

His cheek twitched. Fighting a smile? Or a scowl? "I know all the plots to an eight-book series of regency romances. I'm not even supposed to know what regency romances are."

Perhaps not, but there was something compellingly attractive about a man talking about romances—even if it was to complain.

"I thought you wanted distractions for the Christmas season." She tried for a smile she hoped was endearing.

"And I thought you were offering friendship, not a dating service where I don't even get the option of swiping left or right."

It seemed so out of place, this cowboy in a horse stall, talking about swiping through profiles. "Essentially, you did, though. And Caroline's the only one you swiped ... Which one is good? Left or right?"

"I have no idea. You know why?"

She shrugged.

"Because I didn't sign up for a dating service."

The soft swishes of Pepperjack nosing through the hay indicated the horse's attention had shifted to a snack. Hollis remained focused and inescapable. The most handsome barricade she'd ever faced. If bolting was out of the question, perhaps she could shock him into letting her pass with a kiss.

After all, if it wasn't what he wanted, he'd push her away. Unfortunately, if it was of interest, those strong arms would come around her, and any will to leave would evaporate from her like a winter breath. She'd be more trapped than ever.

Her cheeks burned. "Well, whatever direction it is, it must've worked, because you and Caroline sure looked chummy at the cookie decorating competition." As she brought up the scene yet again, her body tensed. She hadn't wanted to talk about any of this, but hearing out his complaints against her matchmaking didn't feel nearly as awful as focusing on him and Caroline.

He shook his head. "We teamed up as friends. I never asked you to find someone for me."

Friends? Her lungs filled with hope-flavored oxygen. "But you did say you wouldn't mind."

He hooked a thumb on his jeans pocket. "When?"

"I told you about Dolores and Jack, and you confirmed that you want a family and that their little plot didn't bother you."

"*Their* little plot didn't keep landing me in awkward situations."

Odd for someone who looked so at ease to mention awkwardness. With the black hat, calm expression, and athletic build, he had the air of a man who could simply walk away from any situation he didn't want to be in.

She, on the other hand, seemed to get trapped in them like a bug hopelessly stuck to fly paper. "Jack and Dolores are the reason I treated Pepperjack's ulcers. The reason we danced together."

"Were those events awkward for you?"

Her mouth went dry. The dance, especially, had been comfortable. She'd felt sheltered and cared for. And intrigued, especially when he'd talked about his faith. When she'd moved closer—simply to talk without being overheard—she hadn't missed the flash of pleased surprise on his face or the way his hand on her back followed her movement, telling her she was welcome as close as she wanted to be.

"None of that was awkward for me," Hollis said. "At least, not until my *friend* took a personal and secretive interest in my dating life."

"Jack and Dolores put me up to it. They said they wouldn't stop unless I took over matchmaking duties."

"Nobody has more power over you than you give them, Lucy."

Then how would he explain Drake? She opened her mouth, but she couldn't bear to bring her ex into the conversation.

Hollis continued. "As soon as you told me you weren't interested, nothing they did could've forced us into anything, because contrary to what you seem to believe, I have no desire to date someone who isn't interested in dating me."

Oh. Well. Good point. She shrugged helplessly. There it was, that emotion she hated so much, only this time, she could blame no one but herself. Hollis was right, she had given the Carters way too much power.

The corner of his mouth tightened. "For the record, I'm

also not interested in dating someone who doesn't *know* she's dating me."

"I didn't set you up on any dates per se. Nothing was that official."

His lips fixed in a firm line, and he exhaled through his nose. "So what? The plan was to throw Chantal at me next? Is that why you brought her along?"

"No. She was a buffer."

"Between us?"

She shrugged.

A pained line appeared between his brows. "You don't need a buffer with me."

She did, because when he said things like that, she wanted to draw even closer. "You said you wanted to talk. You sounded frustrated. And then there was the whole Caroline thing."

He narrowed his eyes. "What about her?"

If he wanted to make her suffer in return for the game she'd played with his love life, he'd chosen the right punishment. She gulped. "She's a nice person, but no offense, I don't want to hear how in love you are."

His lips shifted with amusement.

Here she'd been hoping he'd argue that he wasn't in love. Who fell in love after one carriage ride and one cookie competition? She raced away in the only way she knew how—conversationally. "Anyway, I'm not sure you can complain about Chantal, no matter why I brought her, Mr. My-Horse-Has-Colic. Obviously, I wasn't the only one with an agenda here."

Pepperjack stirred behind her, but he didn't approach.

"You're right." The gravel in Hollis's voice made her breath catch. "I do have an agenda. Would you like to know what it is?"

Her heart stopped. When he looked at her like that, she did want to know. But mutual attraction—if that's what he was about to confess—terrified her. Would they ride off into a sunset together or over a cliff? She pressed her palm against her breastbone, but the movement stabbed through her wrist. She lifted the offending joint and braced it with her good hand.

"Lucy." Hollis's voice was gently chiding. He dipped his chin and tipped his head to the side as he stepped close. The brim of his hat narrowed her field of vision to his face or their hands. Though calloused, his fingers were gentle as he loosened her hand from around her injury. His feathery touch remained so light as he examined both sides of her wrist, it didn't light sparks of pain. "This is bruising. What happened?"

When he looked into her eyes, waiting for an answer, her throat closed. Her brain took his tipped head and proximity and produced a full-color, surround-sound, 3D movie of what it might be like if he kissed her. A whole pasture's worth of butterflies beat their wings in anticipation.

The intensity of his concern cracked. A faint smile lifted his mouth as his gaze dipped to her lips. But instead of schooling her imagination on what it'd actually be like to kiss him, the smile disappeared, and he lifted an eyebrow. "You're hurt."

She nodded.

"How?"

"Ovation needed his hooves cleaned and checked for thrush, but he didn't want to be caught. He knocked me over when he ran away. I iced it on the way here. It's mild. I'll probably be better in a day or two."

A tendon stood out in Hollis's neck. He released her hurt wrist and placed one hand on her shoulder. The other found her good hand and threaded their fingers together. The small part of her that still wanted to run was quieted by the much larger part of her that hadn't felt so cherished since the dance floor.

"Where was Drake?" he asked.

"Not there. His cousin was somewhere on the property, but I thought I'd have a better chance at earning Ovation's trust alone. I wish you could've been there. Do you think he still trusts you?"

"I don't know." A crease deepened between his brows. "Don't put yourself in danger like that again."

"It wasn't supposed to be dangerous. I have a lot of experience working with animals, and I read up on strategies—"

"Don't put yourself in danger, Lucy. Ever."

She nodded once.

"Is there any way I can convince you to stop going there?"

"To Drake's house? That's where Rosie and Jasmine are. I thought he'd get tired of the game, move on to someone new, and if I could just hang on that long, he'd sell them to me. But it seems he's found a different way to end the game. He's been feeding them corn. I don't know for how long, but I can only think of one reason he'd do that."

"To fatten them for slaughter." Lines bracketed both sides of his mouth.

Her throat stung.

His focus remained intent on her. His expression shifted, but he offered none of his thoughts.

"They're technically livestock." She sniffed and grasped at any fact that might keep her from losing her composure. "I'm not a vegetarian, and I'm not naïve. I treat beef cattle all the time, and I know how it works. But Rosie and Jasmine were petting zoo animals. If not for my involvement with Drake, someone else would've rescued them and given them a good home where they'd get to enjoy the rest of their lives happily grazing in a green pasture."

"You don't know that would've happened." Though quiet, confidence laced his voice.

"They didn't even have the chance at something good

because Drake scooped them up. If not for me, he wouldn't have done that. They're doomed, and there's very little I can do about it except give them the best lives possible in the meantime. Unless I can somehow convince Drake to give them to me."

"They aren't doomed because of you. Same goes for Ovation. We can't control Drake."

"So it's hopeless."

"With God, there's always hope." He waited until she gave a feeble nod. "But I am far more concerned about you than the animals. And I believe God is too. If I could only choose one to save from Drake's clutches, it'd be you. In a heartbeat."

"I'm not in his clutches. I'm free, in a corner of his life by choice because, though it's not life and death for me, it is for Rosie and Jasmine. And maybe even Ovation."

His chest rose with a slow breath. "Are you sure you're as free as you think?"

Hadn't she asked the Lord just earlier today for freedom? Maybe in some ways she didn't have it all figured out. But here, with Hollis's hand around hers, she didn't feel trapped or weighed down. She felt grounded. Safe. And her heart? That galloped, free as could be. "Yes."

"Prove it." He traced her jaw with a finger, then returned his hand to her shoulder.

She lifted her bad hand, meaning to rest it on his chest, but twisting her palm toward him brought pain and she stopped. Maybe she wasn't free. Maybe she was hurt. Her wrist, a shallow representation of a more significant wound.

Hollis closed his hand around hers. He braced the problematic joint straight and comfortable against the rise and fall of his chest. "I can't promise to be perfect, but I do promise to protect you the best I'm able. Have I proven that?"

She nodded.

"I promise to listen to you and to people I trust, even

when they're telling me I'm out of line. *That* was my agenda today. Clint told me I was wrong to spend time with Caroline in hopes of making you jealous. And judging by how ridiculous that sounds when I say it out loud, he was right."

Her eyes widened. "You were trying to make me jealous?"

"Imperfect, remember?"

Lucy chuckled and drew closer.

He released her hand, and his arms encircled her waist. "I promise to admit when I'm wrong and to do all I can to make it right. I promise that if I give you something, whatever it is, it's yours to keep. And I'll never use your capacity for love against you."

Promise after promise wrapped around her aching heart and bolstered it to the point of trust, as solid and real as the man standing before her. When his focus dropped to her lips, her eyes fluttered closed.

A footstep scuffed the floor. "Whoa. Sorry."

At the male voice, Lucy jumped backward. Her wrist banged Hollis's shoulder, and she yelped. Her back pressed against something firm, but before she could melt against the wall, Pepperjack's head loomed beside her own. She'd backed up against his neck, not the wall, and he seemed pleased by the company.

Hollis watched her with an intensity that said he wouldn't have held back from kissing her, even with an audience, if she'd stayed in his arms.

In the hall beyond him, Chantal wrung her hands.

Will, however, grinned. "I'd tell you two to get a room, but I guess you already did. Kinda weird choice though."

Proving the point, Pepperjack withdrew his head and left a trail of slobber on her jacket.

"So, um ..." Chantal's gaze darted toward Hollis, but he paid her no mind. "Do you need help? With the horse, I mean.

Obviously, you wouldn't need help with, um, the other thing." Her face flamed.

"Pepperjack is fine. False alarm." Lucy ducked out of the stall without making eye contact with "the other thing."

She smooshed her hat on and hurried to collect her kit. Not an easy task when she had to put her stethoscope back in, latch it again, and take the handle all with one hand.

She did manage to use her tender wrist to motion toward the exit without inducing a fresh wave of pain. Chantal pivoted and hurried in that direction. Will just kept grinning. She didn't risk a glance at Hollis before she bolted.

Chapter Fifteen

On Sunday morning before church, Hollis steered the truck across the field and over a rise while Will flipped through radio stations from the passenger seat. When he landed on a country station playing Christmas songs, he turned it up. One verse into 'O, Come All Ye Faithful,' Hollis spotted the horses in a loose gathering by the stream that cut through the family land. Hollis put the vehicle in park and reached for his seatbelt.

The song faded from the cab as Will withdrew his hand from the display. "I've been thinking."

After wasting the drive out, now he wanted to talk? The horses were already cantering toward the truck because they knew the vehicle meant fresh hay. Hollis pointed.

"Oh." Will scrambled from his seat.

Hollis met him at the bed and hooked his gloved hands through the twine on the first bale as the horses crowded in. He broke it up to spread it over the frozen ground. He, Frank, and a couple of hired hands had put up the hay this summer to carry the herd through the lean winter months.

If only things weren't lean in more ways than one.

They finished distributing the hay and the mineral buckets that supplemented nutrients the hay didn't provide and met back at the truck.

"You've been thinking what?" Hollis got back behind the wheel. He hadn't planned on needing reverse, but Will had spread hay directly in front of the vehicle, and five horses grazed there.

"Dad left the ranch just as much to me as to you and Mom."

"So you're going to come do your part?" Even as he asked, Hollis sensed the complications.

Will got by as much as required to compete, but he was no brilliant horseman. He didn't have the sensitivity to read the nuance of an animal's behavioral cues. Hollis had watched him crowd a nervous dog and get bitten once. Similar cluelessness had likely inspired the choice to gallop past Brie on the trail ride. He couldn't be involved in training, and even as a ranch hand, he might drive Hollis crazy.

Yet if Will lived at the ranch, he wouldn't need much of a salary, and he could help with the never-ending chores.

Hollis put the truck in reverse, backed away from the herd, and pointed the truck toward the dirt two-track that led to the barn.

"I was thinking I could hire you to work out Edam's kinks." Will rubbed his thumb and index finger together, like he might be nervous.

And he ought to be.

Will couldn't afford the usual rate, so getting Hollis to train Edam wouldn't help Price Quarter Horses.

"Plus," Will continued, "I know a guy whose horse started blowing up in the box. Could use a good trainer, and he might not win all the buckles like you used to, but he's a solid contender. You fix up his horse, that'll count for something."

"One new client isn't going to fix our problems."

"Two clients. I'm one of them. I'll pay you."

Hollis swallowed his skepticism. "I don't need that as much as I need you here, helping with the work."

"Is that really the best use of our time? I mean, you and I together cleaned up at rodeos. We could put the money back into the ranch."

Hollis had made more solo than team roping with Will, but he understood the point. "In the long run, competing again is a possibility, but it won't help enough in time for the private loans we have to pay back in full this summer."

"Oh. So ..."

"We need to prove to a bank that the ranch is a good investment before then, and to do that, we've got to prove that Dad was right about needing the new stable. We have to use it to bring in more than enough to cover the bills."

Will puffed up his cheeks and blew out a long breath. "Then you gotta stop wasting the fact that you're famous. Why don't you have social media? And a YouTube channel? You've practically got the word *trustworthy* branded on your forehead, but doesn't do much good if no one can see it."

"I'm not taking my hat off."

Will snorted. "I'll hang around as long as you need me. Be your cameraman, upload it all for you. Show people a different side of you than the one that other guy keeps smearing all over the internet. Maybe we can get things in shape so you don't have to be here all the time. You could compete again. Get some income that way. Not gonna lie. It wouldn't be bad for me to get my partner back either. You miss it, right? And man, people would love you as a comeback story."

The rodeo flashed in his memory. Applause underscored the excited tones of an announcer. Sweet and savory scents from food vendors' offerings wafted on the air. His mount picked up on the energy. One hand held the calf rope, the other the leather reins. He bit down on the smaller tie-down rope used to secure the calf's legs at the end of the run. With a curt nod, he'd signal, the calf would be released, and instinct—his and his mount's—would take over.

More than any of it, he missed the sense of knowing what he was doing. He missed success. But he'd walked away from that in favor of a life that grounded him. Connected him to Dad. More than that, connected him to something meaningful.

"The rodeo was all about the next seven seconds. Everyone knows their time at the top's limited. You do well enough, they might remember you twenty, thirty years from now, but on the ranch, life's all about the last hundred years and doing what you can to make sure it lasts the next hundred years. It's like working with the generations who've come before us to get ready for the ones that'll come after."

Will shifted and chuckled nervously. "No pressure or anything."

"Say what you want about Dad. Maybe you two didn't click. But this ranch has been good to us." The truck bounced through one last rut, then Hollis steered onto the smoother surface alongside the stable.

"So what you're saying is, this is where you want to raise a family."

Hollis parked the truck and studied the fences and horses that adorned the sloping landscape. "Guess so."

Will's mouth turned into a teasing smile. "Does Lucy know it's that serious?"

Hollis would usually walk away from his brother's antics, but this time he called his bluff by staying put. "When I asked you to keep Chantal busy so I could talk to Lucy, I really thought I'd trusted the right guy with the job."

"So you could romance Lucy in a horse stall with Pepper-jack for a wingman? Come on, man. Even I know better than that."

Remembering the way Lucy's exam had crawled to a stop as her suspicion grew brought a smile. It'd been funny, but romantic? Probably not. Still, she'd ended up in his arms somehow, so maybe it was exactly what their relationship had needed.

"I'll work on it," Hollis said.

Will laughed. "You do that. In the meantime, what do you say? Want to film a 'before' of Edam so we have it for when we post about how good he gets after you're through with him?"

Maybe it would work. It wasn't as if he had a good reputation to ruin. "We can start tomorrow, but you do know that being our videographer doesn't get you out of chores, right?"

"Yeah, yeah. It's my ranch, too."

* * *

Lucy pulled into the lot at Donut Haven on Sunday afternoon. She hadn't been back since the day she'd bolted upon seeing Drake's truck. A flutter of worry batted its wings in her gut as she found a spot. What if he stopped by again?

She pressed ahead because Hollis had asked her to meet him here. Given their interaction yesterday, she had a sense of what he wanted to talk about, and she couldn't let Drake control her any more than he already had. She needed to take the reins of her life back. And once she had them, she needed to steer her life straight toward happiness.

Happiness she might find with Hollis.

She hesitated as she watched other customers come and go from the building.

Hollis was different. He'd proven it many times. She had every reason to believe he'd fulfill each of the promises he'd made to her in Pepperjack's stall yesterday. Even if, technically, he'd lied to her to get her there. After all her matchmaking, she'd deserved the prank. She would've endured worse to hear

Hollis's promises, feel his tenderness, and experience the safety of his arms.

Inside, garland and Christmas ornaments hung from the ceiling. Snowflakes had been sprayed onto the display cases, and the scent of peppermint hung in the air.

Hollis leaned his elbow on the back of a bar-height stool at the counter along the side of the dining room. Whatever was on his phone didn't have his interest hooked, because he spotted her as she walked in and put it away. He met her near the display cases and raised an arm in an invitation for her to come close.

An invitation, not a demand.

When she neared, he greeted her with a side hug. "How's the wrist?"

"Still a little stiff, but nothing like it was when I first fell yesterday."

They got in line, and her thick winter coat swished softly under his fingers as he traced a line up and down between her shoulder blades. "Will you need a table to set things on, or do you want to take our orders to go? We can check out the snow sculptures."

She chuckled as the person ahead of them in line stepped aside. "How much food do you plan to order? I can definitely handle carrying the tea I had in mind."

"We can't stop at Donut Haven without ordering donuts. All of it's my treat, obviously." He pointed to a small case on the counter piled high with beignets. "Those look good. Split an order with me?"

She agreed, and as soon as they reached the sidewalk, he tilted the bag toward her. She picked up one of the pillow-shaped donuts, and he took one for himself.

Even a small bite left her lips coated in sugar. She probably looked like a white-lipped clown. Still, the pastry melted in her mouth and her taste buds hadn't been so pleased with her in ages.

"So do we have a deal?" Hollis asked.

She swallowed the last of her beignet and started cleaning up with a napkin. "A deal?"

He popped the last piece of his in his mouth. It seemed horses weren't the only thing he could expertly control, because not a speck of sugar had stuck to his lips.

He caught her looking and raised an eyebrow.

She shook her head and quickly looked away, only for the pastry bag to appear in front of her.

"Want the last one?"

"It's all yours."

He grunted as if to say, "Suit yourself." A minute later, he dusted his hand with a napkin and stepped away to throw out the empty bag.

When he came back, his steady gaze on her reminded her of the way he'd looked down at her yesterday, as he'd pulled her closer and promised to be trustworthy. "So." He walked close enough beside her that his arm bumped hers. "How about it? Deal?"

"I'm not sure what deal you mean."

He dipped his chin. "I didn't make all those promises yesterday for nothing."

It was only fair for him to want something from her in return. But what promises could she make that would sound half as romantic as his? She'd been so self-focused, she hadn't learned what he needed in a relationship. Aside from the fact that he was sad about his father, of course. She could offer to listen, but that seemed such a small thing in comparison to his vows about safety and love.

Maybe finding out what he needed was as simple as asking. "What do you want in return?"

"A chance."

"That's ... it?"

"Sometimes, that's no small thing." He opened his hand to her.

She fit her hand in his. She could feel his callouses against her palm, attesting to how hard he worked on the ranch. His fingers warmed the back of her hand, and a sense of security seemed to emanate from his grip.

"I think you should ask for more from me," she said.

"Oh?"

"Relationships go two ways, right?"

"Ideally."

"I want ours to be ideal. So you should ask me to promise not to treat you like a project. And of course for the normal things—kindness and empathy and faithfulness."

His hold on her hand tightened. "I don't need to ask when I already know they're guaranteed."

"Given my history, is it really guaranteed I won't keep treating you like a project?"

"Since your project was matchmaking, yes. I'm confident I'll be safe if I can convince you to date me."

* * *

There. He'd said it. Plain and simple. He wanted to date her.

He wanted much more than that too, but he'd figured he'd better start with the minimum. He hoped she felt safe with him in return for how he felt with her: understood, supported, believed in. Or, that was how he felt when it was just the two of them, anyway, not them plus some single woman Lucy wanted to foist on him.

The fact that she held his hand suggested she was willing, but he wanted to hear her say it, and the wait left him feeling as vulnerable as being caught in the open during a hailstorm.

A mischievous smile hooked Lucy's mouth. "You never know. I can be unpredictable."

So could he. He released her hand suddenly, and she turned toward him. Surprise and maybe a tinge of worry replaced her smirk. He held his coffee aside—should've tossed it with the pastry bag—and ran his free hand up her shoulder to the nape of her neck. Her wide eyes flicked to his lips, and she shifted closer.

He leaned in until he could feel her breath brush his chin. "Deal?" he asked.

"Deal."

He kissed her then. Her lips were as soft as he'd imagined, but surprisingly warm, thanks to her tea. Though he wanted to crush her to him and kiss her thoroughly, he brushed his lips against hers gently. Smart and compassionate and maybe a little mischievous, she was exactly the kind of life partner he wanted. If, in their first kiss, he poured out all of that, he'd scare her away for sure. He shifted back, cold air replacing her warmth.

Proving him as guilty of underestimating her as he'd been the morning she'd first filled in as his vet, she hummed a quiet complaint. Her hand, cupping his neck, pulled him back in. Her lips on his returned the kiss and then some, as if she not only sensed but longed for his dreams right along with him. He loosened his hold on restraint, let more of his heart show. If he was right about their potential, this was the start of forever in the making, right there on Main Street for all of Redemption Ridge to see.

Chapter Sixteen

Why did Will filming set Hollis more on edge than all the cameras pointed his way at the rodeo? But if they were going to get out of their financial hole, they needed a new strategy, and Will's idea was the best one they had. There really was something to the power of a family that pulled together.

Not to say it wasn't without its annoyances.

Will had filmed Edam's 'before' footage on Monday. Now, on Tuesday, Hollis worked Edam himself.

Will angled his head to see Hollis around the phone. "You *still* look angry."

"I'm concentrating." Hollis turned Edam away, more to get space from his brother than anything else.

"Do better," Will called after him.

Hollis pasted on an over-the-top smile as he directed Edam back across the indoor arena.

As he got close, he expected Will to complain about the expression. Instead, he said, "You training him was my idea, but I'm still annoyed at how well he listens to you." He rolled his eyes, then tapped the phone screen, presumably ending the clip only after recording his complaint.

Thanks to Will, their videos would have more character than Hollis would have preferred. At least they'd all survived the first training session.

"He has a good base, but he'll take liberties if you're too distracted to correct him as soon as he gets antsy." Hollis hopped to the ground and offered Edam a treat.

"So you're saying I'm the problem."

Only then did Hollis realize Will still had the phone pointed in his direction. He was still on record. "No." He drew out the word as he worked out a positive spin. "I'm saying you can be the solution."

"Hollis Price, ladies and gentlemen." This time, when Will flashed the camera a grin and tapped the screen again, he must've shut it off because he pocketed the device. "I'll edit and upload it tonight. I don't know what this being Christmas week will do to views, but we've gotta start sometime. Maybe people are home, bored and looking for entertainment."

Hollis didn't find time at home boring. There was always something to do around the ranch. Had been since the day he'd moved back. "You seem to know a lot about this. Editing the video?" Hollis wouldn't know where to start.

Will shrugged. "I had it in my head that I could make some money off an online channel. You know if you get enough followers, you get paid for it, right? But it got old before it amounted to anything."

Classic Will. His brother had been helping around the ranch with more than videos, but Hollis knew that might not last long. Or maybe he should have more faith. Will had spent most of his life pursuing roping. The man could stick with a cause when he wanted it badly enough.

Hollis motioned at the phone. "I'm glad for the help. I wouldn't know where to start."

"Finally." Will stood straighter. "Something I'm better at."

"There are lots of things you're better at." Goofing off, falling through ... Hollis handed off Edam. "I have a list of boarding clients' horses to work."

Will started away, and Hollis regretted not trying harder with him.

"We could work the horses together," Hollis called after him. "I could saddle up Pep for you. We could go for a trail ride together, bring two more horses on leads with us."

"Work smarter, not harder." Will kept walking.

Hollis took that as agreement. He checked the exercise logs and chose which horses to take, then headed for Pepperjack's stall to saddle him up first.

As he passed the grooming stall, he heard the quiet sounds of Will grooming Edam. This felt good, working together to make a go of the ranch. Certainly, Mom had been helping all along, but Dad had never wanted her to worry. He would've wanted his sons to band together to find a solution that didn't put more pressure on her.

"I hope you would've been proud of us." Hollis kept his voice quiet to prevent Will from overhearing words meant for their father.

A few steps later, Hollis rolled open Pepperjack's door.

No friendly, pink-tinged nose appeared in the gap. Hollis stepped in.

Pep stood with his head pointed toward the far corner. He made no move to check who'd come to see him.

Hollis's lungs deflated. A glance at Pepperjack's feeder showed the horse hadn't finished his grains or made a dent in his hay. "You all right, buddy?"

He ran his hand along Pepperjack's side. The horse's withers flinched at the contact. Hollis looked in his big, sleepy brown eyes, and nausea threatened.

After calling Lucy in for a case of colic involving a healthy horse, it'd serve Hollis right if he'd simply caught Pepperjack napping and had gotten unduly worked up. But Pepperjack would've eaten before dozing off. He'd had access to this food for hours.

Pep had been going white since his youth and very little gray remained now. A hollow had developed above his eyes, another sign of his age. His muscle mass had decreased, too, in the years since his last rodeo, but his flank was full and round now. Bloated.

Hollis lifted his voice. "Hey, Will?"

"Yeah?"

Hollis didn't have the voice to respond.

A few moments later, his brother appeared in the stall doorway. "Something wrong?"

Pepperjack lifted his upper lip as if to confirm, not that Will could see with the Quarter Horse's head pointed toward the back wall. If only Pep would turn around and bump someone's hat off, Hollis would feel a lot better.

"He's not eating like normal, and see there?" He pointed at Pep's flank.

Will nodded once. "Colic."

The horse huffed—his breathing quicker than Hollis would like—and pawed the ground.

"You could try walking him," Will said.

Hollis nodded. With any other horse, that might be his first move. His prank on Lucy aside, he didn't like to call out a vet over nothing. But this didn't feel like nothing. "I'm going to call Lucy."

"Not Dr. Carter?"

Along the line, Hollis's allegiances had changed. Dr. Carter was good at his job, but to Lucy, Hollis and Pepperjack were more than clients. It was her support he wanted right now.

Will grabbed the halter off the hook. "Make the call. Come find us in the drive when you're done."

Hollis dug out his phone and stepped aside so Will could walk Pepperjack out. As his brother led the horse toward the barn's main entrance, Pep looked back. He might be looking at his side because of pain there. Or he might be looking for Hollis, the one who handled almost all of his care. Either way, Hollis wanted to be there for him. Needed to see his dad's horse through whatever this was. He hit the button to make the call.

* * *

This new barn might be the best haven for horses, but for people, the space could use some improvements. When Lucy determined Pepperjack needed monitoring through the night, Hollis brought out cots. He set one up in the stall and one in the hallway, still neither of them had gotten much sleep. Lucy's body ached by morning, and Pepperjack hadn't improved, despite the treatments she'd administered.

"How long do we wait?" Hollis's rough voice matched the stubble shading his jaw. Seated on the cot in the stall, he took his hat off, scrubbed a hand through his hair, and pressed the hat back on again.

Lucy held the stethoscope to Pep's side once more. His heart rate and breathing were increasing again, and his shoulder twitched whenever she touched him. The last dose of pain meds shouldn't be wearing off already, but they were, and though she had heard some digestion noises when she'd arrived, she didn't anymore.

With a sigh, she turned toward Hollis and spotted Will in the hall behind him. "It's time to take him in."

Hollis nodded once. The line between his brows hadn't eased since she'd arrived, and the skin by his eyes seemed locked in a half-wince. Colic could be life-threatening, and she'd done all she could for Pepperjack here.

"What do you need me to do?" Will asked.

"Hook up the trailer," Hollis instructed. "Pull it around. And let Mom know. She might want to ..." His voice scratched, and his throat pulsed with a swallow. "Come along."

Something told Lucy that wasn't how he'd intended to end the sentence, but Will set off at a jog without question.

She rubbed Hollis's arm. "The referral center will have more options—more tests, closer monitoring. It's still possible they can get things moving again without surgery. And even if they have to operate—"

Pepperjack shifted again and lowered until he sat on his haunches like a super-sized dog.

"Let's get him moving." Lucy clipped a lead to his halter.

Before she could lead Pepperjack from the stall, Hollis's hand brushed hers, taking the lead and ushering Pepperjack out. "Is it safe to transport him like this? What if he rolls in the trailer?"

"I'll medicate him. It's going to be okay." She grabbed the handle on her veterinary kit and pulled it along behind her.

"I don't get how this could happen. We turn him out every day. We haven't changed his diet or his routine. We make sure he gets salt to encourage drinking enough water ..."

She squeezed his shoulder. "Sometimes we never find out. You can do everything right and still run into problems."

Hollis only frowned.

Before she could try harder to convince him not to blame himself, her phone rang. She freed it from her pocket and found Drake's name on the screen. She'd forgotten all about her plans to visit Rosie and Jasmine last night. She lifted the phone to her ear. "I completely forgot I was supposed to meet you. I'm on an emergency call. We'll have to reschedule."

"No need. You're moving on. I thought it time to do the same."

"Moving on? By treating a patient?"

Hollis glanced her way, the grief in his eyes darkened by a new layer of concern.

She made a show of rolling her eyes and shaking her head, trying to tell him he didn't need to worry. At least, not about her. Not now.

"You and Hollis made quite a scene, kissing on Main Street, flaunting your relationship." Drake's voice was light, but if he felt so casual about her connection to Hollis, he wouldn't mention it. "And this after you told me you weren't together. You're making a fool of me, using me to keep your pets, not even bothering to call when you can't make our plans. I'm putting an end to it."

She felt like she was being dragged behind a runaway horse. Her mouth opened but she struggled to form her question. Finally, she said, "What do you mean, putting an end to it?"

"I hear you learned about their diet. I'm sure you can put it together."

"So you have been feeding them corn." Her steps grew heavy with dread. "For how long?"

"Months now. Honestly can't believe you didn't realize it when you found them in the other paddock or when you had to step right over all the signs to go gallivanting out to Ovation."

She replayed the scene in her mind and her false assumption that something else grazed in the pasture, out of sight beyond the rise. Yet the meager evidence she'd seen did point more accurately to a pair of miniature cows than to something larger. How had she failed to see that? "You've been keeping Rosie and Jasmine in that field? Regularly?"

"Why do you think it was so important you make appointments?"

Lucy rubbed her forehead. She'd thought the cows were bulking up. When would she learn to trust her instincts?

"Grass-fed beef just doesn't taste as good, you know?" Drake laughed.

Nausea twisted in her stomach, and she grunted. "Don't joke about things like that."

"Who's joking? I told you, I'm moving on."

The statement wouldn't have hit harder if it'd been delivered via a kicking hoof. She pulsed her jaw, fighting to stay calm. "Explain."

"We're on our way to Polaski's now, so I need to let you go." He grunted. "You should let me go too." He disconnected.

As if she wouldn't have walked out of his life months ago, if not for Rosie and Jasmine. Lucy's phone clattered against the floor.

Hollis broke his stride to scoop it up and hand it back. "What did he do now?"

Pepperjack, who'd lagged behind, stopped too, a big white blur because of the moisture gathering in her eyes. She motioned for Hollis to continue because Pepperjack needed them to—walking would get them closer to the trailer and could help relieve his discomfort, preventing him from rolling where he might hurt himself or anyone standing nearby.

"He's taking Rosie and Jasmine to Polaski's." She clenched her jaw and blinked. Tears fell.

"A butcher?" Hollis's voice was a growl by her side.

She took quick sips of air, the most her lungs seemed capable of processing. Her thoughts lagged too. She could leave to try to talk Drake out of killing her cows after she prepped Pepperjack for transport. At that point, she could do nothing more for Pepperjack anyway, and if she might save her cows, didn't she owe it to them to try? Except going meant she couldn't support Hollis, come what may. It would mean letting Drake control her once again. And after all the times she'd tried and failed to get both herself and the cows away from him, what made her think this time would be any different?

"What do I do?" Her voice came out like a whimper, and she hated the weakness she heard there. *Lord, You're all powerful. What do I do?*

But, of course, it was the man beside her who replied. "I'll handle Drake." His offer was quiet, nearly lost under the thunder of her panic. "Will you stay with Pepperjack? Of the two of us, you're the one he needs right now."

Will rounded the corner at the end of the walkway, headed for them.

She kept pace with Hollis and spoke quickly, trying to get the story out before Will reached them. "Pep only needs me if something goes wrong. But for Rosie and Jasmine, it's already going wrong, and you're the last person who'll get through to Drake. The whole reason he's doing this is because he found out about us. Saw us together, I think. You won't be able to stop him." She darted a glance at Will.

He fell in step with them and took over pulling her kit for her.

Hollis didn't acknowledge him. "Neither can you. Well ..." His focus dipped to the floor. "Unless you're willing to sacrifice us. Even then, if you let him use this stunt to break us up, next he'll use the cows to coerce you into dating him." His jaw pulsed as he lifted his line of sight, sad and serious.

"We're talking about Drake?" Will scoffed. "He's that desperate?"

Desperate wasn't the word she'd use. Evil, maybe. Yet the threat hit like a shark bumping her leg. She could see the situation playing out like Hollis described, and though she knew what that would cost her, she also wasn't sure where to draw the line on saving her cows. She'd built her whole career so she'd never have to let an animal die needlessly.

Whatever power she'd gained, Drake had wrenched from her.

All her work had been useless.

Hollis's statement that people didn't have power over her except what she'd given echoed in her mind. Maybe she'd known that all along, but she'd deemed the sacrifices she'd made worth it to protect her cows.

The truth will set you free.

The truth she hated to acknowledge was that the cows weren't hers. Drake had purchased them. She had gotten attached at his encouragement perhaps, but they weren't her pets. They were his livestock, and he would continue to use them against her as long as she refused to accept that truth.

Perhaps Drake was actually right: She needed to let the cows go to free herself. She'd told Hollis that she had learned to accept the hard parts about her job by trusting God with the things that she couldn't understand or control. With death itself. Were Drake and the fate of the cows in that camp? She pressed a fist to her mouth to block a sob.

Hollis's footsteps hit beats between Pepperjack's clopping hooves. "You said I should ask for more from you."

Her cheeks burned. She deserved a whole laundry list of assignments. What did she know about a healthy relationship?

"I'm asking you, please stay with Pepperjack. Even without me, he'll have family along." He nodded to his brother. "But I'll feel a lot better if you're there for him too. And then I need you to trust me. I will save Rosie and Jasmine from Drake."

"You're not coming to the hospital?" Will asked.

"I don't need to." Hollis's blue eyes stayed intent on her. "Pepperjack is going to be in the best possible hands. Right?"

She blew out a shaky exhale. He'd framed this as a request, a favor she could do him, but the true sacrifice was his own. "I'm not sure I can let you do this."

"If there's gonna be a showdown with the nasty ex, I'm in too," Will said.

Now Hollis looked at his brother.

Will shrugged. "Pep doesn't really know me, but Mom's one of his favorite people, and she'll be out here in a minute. Between her and Lucy, he's covered."

They reached the drive. Will had backed the trailer so the ramp was three feet from the exit. She motioned Hollis to stop and opened her kit to find the medication for Pepperjack. With it in hand, she turned back to find the brothers waiting for her to agree to their plan.

She administered the sedative.

"What's your objection?" Hollis asked from behind her.

She brushed her fingers through Pepperjack's dusty gray mane. "I've never wanted to feel helpless, but he's got me cornered. Either I do nothing, I let him keep controlling me, or I let someone else take over. No matter what, I'm not in control. Powerless."

"Your faith never should've been in yourself or your own power, Lucy." Tenderness softened Hollis's words, but they drew tears, nonetheless.

"It can't be in a man either." She waved a trembling hand at him.

"Two men," Will corrected.

"That's not better." The tears fell. *She* was falling—into despair. If she couldn't get it together, she wouldn't even be able to help Pepperjack. She blinked but her vision swam again immediately.

A strong, calloused hand closed around hers. "Remember our dance? We all need rescue. It comes from God, and sometimes, God puts people in our lives who get to step in when we need them, like I need you now, with Pepperjack. You're not helpless. You're equipped for this. I'm equipped to deal with Drake."

She rubbed her eyes with the heel of her palm. "Then why does he have Ovation?"

Hollis was silent for the space of a breath. Her question had hurt him.

"I'm sorry." She shuddered. He deserved better from her.

His hands tightened around hers, drawing her gaze up as resolve steeled his features. "I'm glad you mentioned him. That gives me an idea. I think Drake might have him for exactly such a time as this."

She didn't know what that meant, but instead of asking, she chose faith. Faith in the goodness of God and in this man, who was so willing to sacrifice for her sake. In faith, she too would do her part. "I'll look out for Pepperjack like he's my own."

Chapter Seventeen

Hollis led Pepperjack into the trailer, praying he'd get to lead the horse back out onto Price Quarter Horses' property again soon. Up until Drake's call, Hollis had felt concern and determination. Now, forced to say goodbye when he longed to stay, he was back in the basement of grief. What if this was the last time he saw Pepperjack? What if he lost this piece of his dad for good?

He raked his sleeve across his eyes, grateful the trailer walls blocked the others from witnessing the emotions that were slipping from his hold like a rope he hadn't secured to the saddle horn. Leaving Pepperjack in a crisis felt like betraying not only an animal that had been nothing but good to him, but also his dad. As if he wasn't already failing Dad enough by running the business into the ground.

Pepperjack looked so sleepy and weak. And Hollis was just supposed to leave him like this?

He ran his hand down the horse's warm neck. "Lucy's going to take the best care of you. You're better off with her than with me, trust me."

Pep only blinked.

What Hollis wouldn't give to have the horse knock off his hat and trample it in a show of Pep's hallmark spunk. But even in his hazy state, the horse could be sensing Hollis's ragged emotions. Those wouldn't help him feel any better. Hollis sniffed and exhaled long and slow, trying to get himself together.

"I don't know what I'm doing." Hollis kept his voice low, as he always did for these secret, one-sided conversations. "Is this the right choice, Dad? Because it feels like walking out on family, and isn't family supposed to come first?"

"You'd be better off asking the Lord questions like that one."

Hollis dropped his chin. He hadn't heard his mom join him and Pepperjack in the trailer. She was right. Hollis had tried to talk to his dad about a lot of things when he should've been talking to the Lord this whole time. Still, it wasn't easy when the Lord had said no to the last big thing Hollis had asked for—his dad's healing.

Hollis sighed. Anger might be a normal part of the process, but it sure did lead him to dead ends.

Dad wasn't still sick in heaven. Hollis knew that. Knew the way the situation had played out shouldn't leave him resenting the Lord, who'd blessed him in so many ways, including with the promise that he'd one day be reunited with his dad.

Mom smoothed a hand across his shoulders. "But if you mean choosing to leave Pep to me and Lucy while you see to other matters, your dad would be proud of you."

His eyes flooded faster than a canyon during a thunderstorm. Dad wouldn't be proud of how Hollis was losing the ranch. "If you knew ..." He shook his head. Why confess the financial problems now?

"Will's chatty. You know that, right?" Mom sighed. "I know everything, and I think I know why you didn't feel you could tell me. Because you were raised by your father, who prioritized this family and our ranch. But make no mistake, family didn't come first for him. Not quite. God did. I'm sure you've noticed by now, family lets us down sometimes. It's the Lord who won't."

Hollis lowered his head and nodded. He shouldn't have needed the reminder—his dad had raised him better—but he appreciated it nonetheless. Somewhere along the line he had let his priorities slip out of their proper order.

His mom squeezed his shoulder. "If you think the Lord is prompting you to go put a bully in his place, especially when you know Pepperjack couldn't be in better hands, you should go. Same choice your dad would've made. A hundred times over. In fact, I think if forced to choose between having not just one horse, but the entire ranch as his legacy or your loyal streak, he would want the loyalty passed on." She patted Pepperjack. "Leave him to us."

Faith meant even more than family, and loyalty meant more than the ranch. Yet the Lord had also granted for it all to work together. Hollis wasn't betraying Pepperjack, because Pepperjack would have others for support.

He'd always known he wasn't meant to run the ranch alone. Maybe that was why he'd had such a hard time letting go of his dad. But even without him, he had God first, then Will and Mom, ready and willing to do their part. Together, they could carry on the traditions that had supported their family for generations. And even if they did fail, they had something better.

Thanks to hope anchored not in this troubled world but, instead, in a secure eternity, impossible goodbyes became just bearable enough to utter.

"Love you, Pep." He patted Pepperjack one last time, then squeezed his mom's shoulder. "And I love you too."

They stepped out of the trailer and onto the drive.

She patted his cheek, then turned to Lucy. "Ready?"

Lucy swallowed hard but nodded. She started to turn away, but Hollis stepped into her path and pulled her into an embrace. When they parted, her smile was devastatingly sad, but her choice to climb in the passenger seat and leave with his mom spoke even more powerfully of her choice to trust both him and the Lord.

Though he couldn't say what outcome the Lord would give them, Hollis would do everything in his power to make sure her trust in him wasn't misplaced.

Will rubbed his hands together. "What are we going to do to Drake?"

* * *

Hollis parked his truck outside Ridgeline Grill and paused to pray yet again that the Lord would grant him favor—more favor than He already had when Ken Polaski agreed to a stay of execution and told Hollis and Will where to find Drake.

"You still haven't told me the plan," Will said.

"Just don't let me punch him."

Will's eyebrows lifted. "Is that a risk?"

Hollis wasn't normally one to lose his temper, but he hated what Drake had been doing to Lucy. Hated that he'd tried to split them up. Hated that he'd threatened the lives of two fluffy cows Lucy loved so much—an attachment Hollis understood better now that he'd glimpsed the creatures at Polaski's. Not that Hollis would go to all this trouble just for them. But for Lucy? And to stop Drake's reign of tyranny over her, the cows, and Ovation? He'd do this and more.

"You sure you want me to stop you?" Will said. "What if he—"

"Will."

His brother lifted a hand as if taking a vow. "Violence is not the answer."

That'd have to do. He headed inside, Will at his heels. Having this conversation in public should keep Drake from twisting the truth. Since his reputation mattered to him, he might respond more reasonably to Hollis's first offer so he wouldn't have to resort to the riskier idea.

He hadn't expected much of a crowd for lunch on Christmas Eve, but two couples and a family all waited to be seated by the hostess station. Hollis walked right by and into the dining area. Guests occupied most tables. Staff hurried to clear the empty ones for the next set of diners while wait staff collected orders and delivered meals and drinks.

Drake sat at one of the larger tables with a group of professionals, all dressed for a business meeting. Shortly after Hollis had moved home, when he'd worked alongside his dad, they'd sold some horses to one of the men for use on his ranch. Hopefully, this dinner celebrated the close of his business with Drake. Hollis wasn't out to sour plans for anyone besides Drake. And even in that case, he hoped to do this as painlessly as possible.

Hollis's former customer noticed him and nodded a greeting.

That signaled Drake to turn.

Hollis met him with the first of the offers he'd planned, one that sounded generous, though it was actually a fair trade. "I'll buy you twice as much beef as you'd get off those two tiny heifers if you'll give them to me." A live mini Highland cost about the same as a full share of beef off a full-sized animal.

"Too late. I dropped them at Polaski's an hour ago. They said they'd get right to work."

"Not everyone's comfortable butchering people's pets. Ken's one of them. He couldn't believe you'd want a part in a nasty business like that either."

Drake placed his napkin on the table and rose. "You didn't seriously come to a restaurant that specializes in steak"—he spoke slowly and intoned the statement like a lawyer trying to tear apart a witness on the stand—"on the grounds of a working cattle ranch to argue that cattle should be treated as pets." He looked around as if inviting the restaurant full of people to laugh.

No one did.

"Those two should be, because that's what they are to Lucy. What'll it take to buy them off you?"

Drake snorted and shook his head. "They aren't for sale."

"How about twenty grand?"

Will coughed, and Hollis assumed it was a protest, but a fair price had already failed to work. Hollis had the money in savings. The trouble was, the more he spent on the livestock, the less he'd have for the ranch to fall back on. But he didn't have enough to save the ranch anyway, if they couldn't secure a new loan. He might as well use what remained of his money for something good.

Besides, if he was going to operate under the belief that he wasn't alone and that loyalty mattered more, then he didn't need to hoard his resources. The Lord would provide.

"They are not for sale. Especially not to the likes of you. After what you did to Ovation, those cattle are better off never setting foot on your ranch."

Perfect. He'd hoped Drake would bring Ovation into this. "Sixty grand for Ovation and the cattle."

Drake's eyes widened, the first sign that Hollis had piqued his interest, but a sneer quickly took over. "What do you think this is, an auction?"

Will edged into his line of sight, a silent look of warning on his face. Probably didn't want Hollis to bid any higher.

"Take the money and run," someone at the table quipped.

Drake adjusted the lapels of his suit jacket. "I don't just *say*

Ovation is unrideable. It's a fact. The video's all over the internet. Your girlfriend practically got trampled trying to clean his hooves."

"I saw that horse in person," a man at a nearby table said. "Beautiful, but crazy. Dangerous, even."

The benefits of having this out in front of a small-town crowd, where everyone knew everyone.

"Then sixty thousand is considerably more than he's worth, even with the cows thrown in."

"You are wasting my time and interrupting our dinner. Not to mention disturbing everyone else." Drake motioned to the tables around them.

Most of the diners peered in their direction.

"We're enjoying the show," someone said from Drake's own table.

"Sounds like a good deal, Drake," another voice added.

"It's not about the money." Drake turned his head but didn't pivot all the way to face whoever had weighed in. "It's about the principle."

Hollis had suspected as much, and he'd come prepared with a plan to play into that principle.

Cassie Keen, who was part owner of this ranch and the restaurant, headed their way. Back in the day, she'd worked on the rodeo circuit, and they'd interacted some, but Hollis wasn't sure he had enough goodwill stocked up with her that she'd let him use her dining room as a stage.

"And the principle is that I treat animals so poorly, I shouldn't have them?"

Drake shrugged. "You said it."

"How about a wager?"

Drake crossed his arms and cocked his head.

"If I can saddle and ride Ovation without him attempting to throw me, you'll sign over all three animals to me."

Drake scoffed. "For free?"

"You said it wasn't about the money." Hollis resisted a glance her way, but Cassie was almost to them, and they'd have to take this conversation away from the audience he hoped would pressure Drake into the deal. "If you're right that I ruined Ovation, it shouldn't matter, anyway. I'll never be able to ride him."

Drake glared, assessing Hollis. They both knew Hollis hadn't ruined Ovation. What neither of them could know in advance was whether Ovation would still trust Hollis enough to let him ride. The way Ovation had plowed by Lucy suggested he'd lost a lot of trust since his time at Price Quarter Horses, where Ovation had been a model client for the farrier. Hollis probably should've consulted Clint, a pro at rehabilitating horses, before issuing the challenge, but Hollis could think of no other offer Drake would accept. If Drake accepted the terms, Hollis would spend the drive over to Hasting's place on the phone with Clint.

"There a problem here, boys?" Cassie propped one hand on her hip, shoulders back with relaxed confidence.

Hollis gave her a tight smile.

Drake ignored her. "I'll give you one hour."

"Two hours. I hear I need to clean and check his hooves for thrush first."

Drake's jaw ticked, because an untreated bacterial infection signaled he'd been lax about his horse's care. "I had someone out to try. Ovation wouldn't cooperate."

"So we have a deal?" Hollis asked.

"What've you got to lose?" The rancher Hollis and his dad had worked with pushed up from his place at the table. "I don't know about the rest of you, but I'm curious if the younger Price has the same skills his father did."

With a shrug, another of the diners stood. A third motioned over a waiter, presumably asking for the check. Hollis had wanted a crowd, and it looked like he'd have one.

Drake glared. "An hour and a half. You have to ride him a full circle around his enclosure. If he bucks or rears up once, deal's off."

Hollis nodded, already praying the Lord would calm Ovation the way he'd once calmed lions for Daniel.

Hollis's former customer slapped Drake on the shoulder. "We'll be in the market for another horse this spring, and I gotta know if what you've been telling us about Hollis here is right." The guy ambled toward the door.

With that, it seemed more than Ovation, Rosie, and Jasmine's futures were on the line. If Hollis could prove himself, he could rescue the animals and reassure clients who'd been scared off by Drake's claims about the quality of his work. If he failed, he'd lose it all—the animals, the ranch, and Lucy's trust.

Lord, be with us.

Chapter Eighteen

Lucy paced and prayed. Waiting for results was so much worse than being the one running the tests and administering treatment. She'd called ahead to the referral center and described Pepperjack's situation, so staff had been ready to admit him when they arrived. The old gelding was in back now, where they were likely repeating the diagnostics Lucy had done as well as tests that hadn't been possible in the field.

"What in the world?" Susan's muttered question halted Lucy's pointless circles.

She sank into the waiting room chair beside Hollis's mom, who peered at her phone.

On screen, a video played. Hollis held his arms out while Drake patted him down, as if looking for weapons.

"What's in your pocket?" Drake demanded.

"Chopped up carrot." Hollis dug out the pieces and showed them to Drake, who checked the coat pocket again. "I never agreed to do this without rewards."

Instead of replying, Drake motioned him to go ahead.

"Now that it's been determined that Hollis doesn't have

tranquilizers on him, it's time for the show to begin." The off-screen narration was unmistakably Will, mimicking the tone of a rodeo announcer. A red box in the corner of the screen indicated this was streaming live. "For ownership of the horse in question and a pair of mini cows, Hollis Price needs to clean the hooves and ride a horse the owner claims is unrideable in the next hour and a half. Time begins when he enters through the gate."

Hollis approached the fence. Tack had already been set on the rails, ready for use. Hollis collected a halter and lead rope, let himself into the pasture, and whistled. "Ovation, come here." Now that he was farther from the camera, a breeze muffled his voice, but the horse obviously heard him because he trotted forward.

Lucy's breath caught. Could it be that easy?

About ten feet off, Ovation halted, shook his head, and circled away. A jeer rose. Hollis ignored it and tried again.

And so went the dance, forward and backward, closer and farther.

Susan sent Lucy the link, and she watched from her own phone as Ovation's retreats lessened. Hollis's voice quieted, and Lucy could no longer hear what he said, but she could see the horse's ears pricked toward him, hanging on every word, responding to every movement.

When Ovation accepted a slice of carrot and let Hollis put the halter on, Lucy's eyes misted and she thanked the Lord. The sound of a few subdued claps carried over her phone. Hollis had managed in ten minutes what had taken her four times as long. The man had a gift. A connection with that horse.

A connection that was about to be tried.

Ovation didn't charge when Hollis went to clean his hooves, but he also didn't stand still. When the dancing around interfered with the job, Hollis walked the horse backward and tried again. Ovation still fidgeted. Hollis backed him up some more.

Lucy wasn't sure why that worked, but eventually, Ovation stood still, and Hollis got to work cleaning his hooves.

"Susan Price?" At the female voice, Lucy's attention jerked away from the phone.

Susan rose. "That's me."

The clinician's apologetic smile told Lucy before she said another word that Pepperjack's situation was serious. "We'd like to evacuate the impaction surgically."

Lucy stood and put an arm around Susan. Since both of her sons had gone to help Lucy, she needed to at least offer what comfort she could. Yet, Susan remained composed. She tracked what the doctor said, asked questions, and with a steady hand signed the paperwork.

The doctor bustled away again, and Susan turned toward her. "Well, what do you think?"

"A horse that's in general good health like Pepperjack has a good prognosis. Once he's home again, I'll come by and check on him often so nothing will be left to guesswork."

Susan nodded. "Thank you. He is a special horse, and I'm praying hard that everything goes well here. But I meant, do you want to head back? You got him here safely, and he's out of our hands now. We might be able to get to Hollis before his time runs out with Ovation."

Oh. Right. She still held her phone, but the screen had gone dark.

Unfortunately, no matter how much reason they had to believe Pepperjack would do well through the surgery, they couldn't be sure it would go without complication. Susan shouldn't be an hour away.

Though Hollis's commitment to save her cows—or try to, anyway—made her choice easier, she had ultimately surrendered the cows to the Lord. She still couldn't be sure how the Lord would cause the situation to work out, but if her surrender was her act of faith, she needed to stay the course. "Let's stay here in case Pepperjack needs us."

* * *

Ovation tugged backward when Hollis led him toward the fence where he'd left the saddle and bridle. Drake glowered at them from the little crowd. Not only had Drake's dinner company followed them out, but others had straggled in afterward, probably as word spread through town about the deal they'd struck.

First Jason Keen, Cassie's husband and a former rodeo star himself, came with his father-in-law, rancher Barry Reynolds. Hollis didn't know either of them well enough to say if they'd come to support either Hollis or Drake or out of simple curiosity.

Some showed their allegiances by who they chose to stand beside. Clint, Cody, and Neenah had gathered near Will. A man Hollis didn't know took up station beside Drake. Those two were the loudest of the bunch, quick to criticize whenever Ovation got nervous. Every time Drake lifted his voice, Ovation got antsier. Hollis had managed to clean out Ovation's hooves and treat the thankfully mild thrush he'd found, but walking the horse right up to Drake to tack him up wouldn't do.

Hollis stroked Ovation's almost black nose. "What do you think? Will you wait here for me?"

Ovation shifted.

Hollis checked the time. It was passing quicker than he'd like, but they still had half an hour. He could walk the horse farther away and tie him to a different section of fence to wait and be saddled, but Drake might walk down and spook

Ovation there too. Hollis dropped the lead and continued alone to collect the tack. If he had to catch the horse again, so be it.

Hollis looped the bridle over his shoulder and hefted the saddle and saddle pad into his arms. When he turned back, he almost laughed with relief that Ovation had stayed put, but once he got within ten feet, Ovation tossed his head and trotted off.

Hollis couldn't blame him. During the horse's time with Drake, tacking up meant bracing for mistreatment. When Hollis collected Ovation's tack from the barn, he'd made Drake swap out his bridle for the one Hollis had used with him at Price Quarter Horses. Drake had said Ovation would never behave with the gentle bit Hollis preferred. Just another sign of what Drake had put his horse through.

Hollis was asking Ovation for a lot with today's challenge. More than he ought to ask from a mistreated horse. Thanks to a hurried phone call, Clint had given him advice on the way over, but he'd also warned him it was possible Ovation wouldn't come around as quickly as Hollis needed.

Hollis prayed for the Lord to fill in the gaps with heavenly discernment. His dad's voice came back to him from across the decades, when they'd first been training Pepperjack. "We're gentling, not forcing."

Hollis set the saddle on the ground, balanced standing up and leaning on the pommel, and draped the saddle pad and bridle over it. Hands free, he walked away from the tack and called Ovation.

The horse came. Hollis led him back to the saddle, gave another treat. Ovation didn't protest about the saddle pad, but when Hollis lifted the saddle onto his back, he pranced sideways.

"Whoa. You're okay. You're all right." Hollis spoke low and calm until Ovation settled. A few treats later, he tied the cinch. Meanwhile, Ovation held his breath with his ribs expanded. Hollis chuckled at the tactic to keep the saddle loose. "This isn't my first rodeo, buddy."

Still, he let it go and swapped the halter for the bridle. Ovation didn't make it easy, but once Hollis got it on, Ovation chomped a couple of times then stilled, like he already recognized the difference in bit before any pressure had been applied.

Showtime.

Hollis returned to the saddle, snugged up the cinch, and put a foot in the stirrup. Ovation stood still. Hollis lifted himself off the ground, but before he could get a leg over, Ovation shifted away. Hollis barely got his seat before Ovation jolted forward.

"Whoa." He sat back in the saddle and pulled the reins. "Whoa. We have time. Easy."

Ovation nodded. The movement indicated uneasiness rather than agreement, but the horse did slow into the walk Hollis asked for. They reached the fence a good thirty feet from the closest spectator, and Hollis directed Ovation to follow the rails away from the crowd. They'd save crossing in front of Drake for last, and with any luck, someone would convince the guy to back away before they got there.

Though he was bound up with tension Hollis could feel through the saddle, Ovation responded to gentle directions that kept him near the fence. If Drake had a lighter hand or a less sensitive horse, maybe they would've been all right together. Then again, as Hollis had tended to Ovation's hooves, he saw the scars from being trained without the proper gear. Ovation had many reasons for wanting to get Drake off his back—literally.

"Those days are over," Hollis vowed.

Ovation's ears swiveled toward him, listening, so Hollis

kept up a conversation that wasn't one-sided because the horse responded by relaxing his bunched-up muscles.

Their easy walk gave Hollis plenty of time to look around. Cattle grazed beyond Ovation's paddock. The snowcapped mountains fenced in the property, and a stream trickled over a rocky riverbed, providing water for Ovation and the pasture beyond. They turned to the third side of the enclosure, which pointed them back toward Drake's house, a modern build with generous windows.

The house at Price Quarter Horses had about a hundred years on this one. It'd been built more for function than luxury, and Hollis wouldn't trade it.

"Come to think of it, you'll have fancier digs than me, if we can keep this up." He patted Ovation's withers.

The horse kept walking. Hollis checked the time. They'd used most of what they'd been given, but they were on track to finish with a couple of minutes to spare. Of course, he'd rather finish sooner than later, but asking Ovation to pick up the pace risked upsetting the rhythm they'd settled into. Better to see this through at a walk. Once Ovation was his, he would enroll him in Clint's program until he was well enough to undergo another round of roping training to shore up the skills Drake had eroded.

Then, he'd find a roper in need of a solid horse. Hopefully, one willing to pay what Ovation was worth.

They made the last turn and headed back up the rail that would lead them past their audience. Will stood farthest back, where Hollis and Ovation had first met up with the fence, waiting for them at the finish line with his phone up. Probably recording the whole thing for posting online later if Hollis succeeded.

Closer, between Hollis and his goal, stood Drake and his buddy. They leaned on the rails with their hands hanging over. Drake held his hat in hand, and one wrong move with it could startle Ovation. Still, the challenge had been to ride the entire perimeter within an hour and a half of setting foot in the pasture.

Only then did he realize Lucy and his mom would've reached the vet a while ago. Treatment decisions had likely been made, but he'd left his phone with Will. What if they'd already reached out with bad news? Grief stabbed his chest, sudden and sharp, and Ovation grunted nervously.

Hollis shook out his shoulders and replayed what his mom had said. The Lord wouldn't fail, no matter what they faced. Hollis couldn't control the outcomes for Pepperjack, the ranch, or the training business. But none of that was the legacy he was responsible for. The legacy was loving loyalty. Right now, living that out meant keeping his mind on the task at hand: securing Ovation, Rosie, and Jasmine's futures.

"He's supposed to be trained as a roping horse," Drake's buddy said. "Not a fairground pony ride."

Hollis felt Ovation's back tense. "They can't touch you, buddy."

The bunched-up muscles didn't relax, and his gait turned choppier.

For the horse's sake, for Jasmine and Rosie, for Lucy, Hollis willed his voice to stay calm and the tension in his own body to evaporate, because if he could sense the horse's unease, the horse would pick up on any hint of it from him. "We're almost home free. You're going to be all right. Just a few more yards."

"This is ridiculous." Drake jerked back from the fence and swung his hat up onto his head.

Ovation went into reverse, one step, two. Hollis steered him away from Drake and circled back. But once they returned to the fence, Ovation refused the cue to move forward and try again.

"Come on, buddy." The horse pranced sideways, chin tucked to his arched neck.

"Get away from the fence." Clint's call was directed at Drake.

"You're forgetting whose property this is," Drake returned.

Ovation's composure cracked further, and Hollis steered him in a tight circle to keep him from bucking. Drake wouldn't move, and they'd run down the clock getting to this point. Not only did he not have time to coax Ovation past Drake, he wasn't sure he'd be able to do it from the horse's back.

Dad would know what to do, but as his mom had pointed out, Hollis would be better off praying than asking questions of a father who could no longer answer him. *What now, Lord?*

Ovation pulled out of the turn and trotted away from his nemesis.

Peace, as unexpected as the grief had been, dropped over Hollis. Not usually how he responded to a horse ignoring an instruction, but this was the answer—ride Ovation the opposite direction around the pasture, using Drake as a new start and finish line. They'd have to book it to make it around in time, but one subtle cue from Hollis sent Ovation into a canter.

The horse loped around the back portion of the pasture as Hollis wondered at what had just happened. He'd made such a habit of talking to his dad this year, he'd let the habit of prayer falter. Yet if Dad's legacy was one of loyalty, how much more so was God's? Despite the way Hollis had reacted to his dad's death, his heavenly Father still showed His love and waited for him to respond.

They rounded the last turn. Down the fence line, Drake stalked their direction. To complete the challenge, Hollis needed to get Ovation past him.

After a split-second prayer, Hollis gave Ovation a squeeze.

The quick, bumpy cadence of the canter stretched into a smooth, thundering gallop. The landscape smeared. The speed would either give Ovation less time to succumb to fear or provide that much more momentum with which to throw Hollis off his back. Either way, he egged Ovation on, and they flew over the terrain.

Hollis didn't go deaf to the cheers of his friends. He didn't lose sight of Drake, standing slack-jawed at the fence. If he could track it all, Ovation could too. The horse knew he was galloping toward the man who'd scarred him. Yet Ovation didn't break his stride, and then Drake was behind them in every way that mattered.

Hollis guided Ovation around in a wide circle, slowing the pace until they were walking in the middle of the field. The spectators continued cheering, and Will still had his phone up, recording. Amazing the guy's battery hadn't died yet. Did he plan on filming the whole cooldown?

The gate opened, and a woman stepped into the pasture, tall and slender with long hair falling around her shoulders from under her hat. Lucy. Lucy was here?

What did that mean about Pepperjack?

She broke into a run toward him, and he dismounted, unsure whether he ought to be celebrating or grieving. But even Lucy's hurried pace couldn't disguise her grin. That joy ruled out the worst possibilities, and Hollis heard himself laugh.

As she got near, Ovation tugged away from her advance. Lucy pulled up short, and Hollis turned his attention to the gelding.

"You did it, buddy. You're home free now."

Ovation stopped pulling, but he kept his head high, on alert.

"Easy, there." Clint's voice came from behind him, then he stepped up beside Hollis. "I can take him from here."

"You good with that?" Hollis studied the horse. Ovation was still on edge, but he wasn't struggling to bolt from Clint's presence. He handed over the reins.

"Let's go for a walk, buddy." Clint stepped backward. Ovation trailed him, hesitantly at first and then more easily.

As soon as the pair passed Lucy, she launched forward and wrapped her arms around Hollis. "That was amazing. I'm so proud of you." She pulled back just enough to look up into his eyes. "So they're all ours now?"

Ours? As much as he wanted that, he shook his head. "The cows are yours. But they have a home at Price Quarter Horses as long as you want them there."

She laughed, pulled him in for a quick, grateful kiss, and then her big eyes peered up at him again. "And Ovation is yours! Right? That was the deal?"

"It was." Though she was pretty well-informed for someone who was supposed to have been at a surgical center an hour away. "And Pepperjack?"

Her joy dampened. "He's in surgery. Your mom stayed, but she insisted there was nothing more I could do for him, so I needed to come back for this. To see you in person."

He tightened his arms around her. "I'm glad you're here."

"It's much better than just watching online. We'll have to go pick up your mom, but that'll also give us the chance to check in on Pepperjack after he wakes, which I figured you'd want either way."

"Yes. Absolutely. But, um, watching online?"

"Will's been streaming everything. I can't wait to go back and watch the parts I missed while I was driving, but he's a surprisingly good play-by-play announcer. He might've missed his calling."

Beyond Lucy, Will now stood in the open gate, his phone in hand.

"He played it live?" A risky decision that sounded exactly like Will.

Lucy nodded. "He read off some of the comments that were coming in. It sounds like people really respected the way you worked with Ovation here. This might be all the help your reputation needed to rebuild—"

"Is he still streaming?" Hollis suspected he knew the answer because Will headed toward them with the phone up.

Lucy glanced over her shoulder and shrugged. "Probably. Why?"

"If people have been watching this whole time, we'd better make sure we don't disappoint our audience."

"Disappoint ...?" Lucy's question trailed off when he cupped her chin and leaned in.

The brims of their hats bumped, and he took his off, held it like a shield next to their faces.

Lucy laughed. "I thought we had an audience to please."

He nuzzled her cheek. "They'll get the idea."

Her eyes lit, and her pleased exhale brushed his lips.

He closed the distance. For a moment, he could track his surroundings—some cheers from the fence line, Will complaining about the PDA, his responsibilities related to Rosie, Jasmine, Ovation, and Pepperjack. But as he held Lucy and felt her respond to the kiss, it all fell away.

They'd chosen each other over grief, over trying to control outcomes themselves, and over self-protective actions that would have driven them apart. This, their reward, was so much better than what he bargained for when he first agreed to be friends with one Dr. Lucy Aveline for the Christmas season. The Lord had given them both healing and their very own shot at happily ever after in each other's arms.

As Hollis neared the stable, a familiar laugh bubbled over the springtime twitter of birds. He dropped from the saddle and led his mount toward the noise. Lucy perched on a hay bale, scrubbing her fingers through Jasmine's fluffy coat. Jasmine thanked her by licking her cheek clear up to her hairline. Meanwhile, Rosie pranced around and tossed her head, trying to rid herself of a hunk of hay bale she'd hooked with her horns.

Pepperjack's white nose appeared in Hollis's peripheral vision, then his hat flipped from his head. Hollis caught it, snorted, and led the horse to the fence closest to Lucy. She still hadn't spotted him.

Rosie ditched the hay and stomped on it victoriously, and Lucy cheered for her. The coppery cow zoomed away, and Jasmine popped to her feet, far more agile than a creature shaped like a TV stand ought to be.

Lucy laughed again, and Hollis couldn't help chuckling.

He much preferred the company of horses to the companionship of cows himself, but Lucy's joy with this pair of animals proved contagious. No wonder Drake hadn't given this up willingly.

Thank God for the circumstances that had forced the man to surrender.

After Hollis's ride, Drake claimed Ovation reared up toward the end, when Drake startled the horse with his hat. Will's video proved otherwise. The client Drake had been wining and dining held him to account, saying he'd heard the deal plain as day and he was sure Drake would honor his word.

He did. Ovation went with Clint for rehab, and Lucy and Hollis swung by Polaski's for the cows.

By that point, Pepperjack came safely through surgery. They arrived at the surgical center just as staff allowed him visitors. Hollis managed a couple of other visits during Pep's eight days at the facility, but throughout that time, his schedule got busier and busier with new clients eager to hire him.

With Hollis's time monopolized by training, Will led the care and maintenance of the ranch and its herd. They still posted videos regularly. Their most recent one, about Ovation's graduation from rehab and roping school, had already generated some potential buyers just days after it'd gone live.

Praise the Lord, he, Will, and Mom were going to be okay. The ranch would be. Ovation, too. He still missed Dad, but all the answers to prayer he'd seen these last few months reminded him that even that loss wasn't forever. God would one day grant them a reunion, and in the meantime, the Lord had blessed him with a beautiful life.

Lucy turned toward him, and her full lips pulled into a perfect smile. She waved with both hands and sidestepped a pile of manure to approach the fence.

"I didn't know you were coming," he said. "We would've waited for you."

Pepperjack nickered as she neared.

Her expression melted, and she pressed a hand to her heart, eyes on the horse. "You sweet thing." She ran her hand along Pep's jaw and kissed his nose before turning her princess eyes on Hollis. "I couldn't resist stopping by to see how your first ride went. Everything good?"

"Except that there's an electric fence between us."

She laughed again.

He'd spend a lifetime trying to keep her this happy, this full of laughter.

She hurried off to the gate and let herself through, but Hollis froze on that thought—the vow to make her happy for a lifetime. He didn't have a ring to back it up yet, but he harbored no doubts about where they were headed. Could it be they'd only known each other—really known each other— five months now? Yet a lifetime commitment didn't daunt him.

She reached him, and her hand smoothed across his chest. "How's this? Better?"

He leaned in for a kiss, but she pulled back.

"You probably don't want to do that. Jasmine just licked me."

"She only got your cheek."

Her eyes glinted. "That you saw."

He hesitated, but ... nope. Couldn't dissuade himself. If it was good enough for Lucy's lips, it was good enough for him. He won on the gamble—she tasted of vanilla lip balm.

"I love you, *Dr.* Lucy."

She pressed a kiss to his jaw, and her words breezed softly to his ear. "You can call me Lucy."

"Can I?" He pulled back enough to study her.

Bright sunlight danced in her eyes. "I love you too, Hollis."

He kissed her again, slow and thorough.

"I've never been so happy to lose a client," a man said.

"But of course, I knew that was the risk when I sent Lucy out here."

Lucy pulled away. Probably the proper thing to do, but Hollis barely suppressed his groan.

Jack Carter crossed the drive, headed their way. Had he been here the whole time, in the house, perhaps? Or had he driven up while Hollis had been focused on Lucy? "I don't know which I should be happier to see, that Pepperjack is doing well post-surgery or that our matchmaking worked after all."

Lucy bit her bottom lip. A grunt caught in Hollis's throat.

Jack stopped in front of them, hands on his hips, grinning. "That is, I assume he's doing well."

Hollis motioned for Jack to see for himself. "Lucy just cleared him for rides yesterday, so I took him out for a short one. He did great."

"And the matchmaking?" Jack's amused gaze bounced from one of them to the other. "That must've gone well."

Lucy's face turned as red as a setting sun. Was she that bashful about her dating life or just embarrassed about her awkward attempts at setting Hollis up?

He took her hand and squeezed. "Let's just say, I'm glad I never have to go through that again."

Jack cocked his head. "No?"

Lucy's eyes darted toward him too.

What he'd said did have some implications, didn't it? Well, so be it. He'd been thinking in lifetimes. Might as well start talking that way too. "I've met my match."

Ready for more?

Christmas in Redemption Ridge Series

Year 1
Marrying the Rancher's Daughter
(Jason and Cassie)
By Tara Grace Ericson

Remembering the Rancher
(Maverick and Annabella)
By Liwen Y. Ho

Year 2
Amending the Christmas Contract
(Levi and Ruby)
By Hannah Jo Abbott

Wooing the Widower
(Chaz and Margie)
By Elle E Kay

Year 3
Dreaming About Forever
(Jordan and Alicia)
By Mandi Blake

Bidding on a Second Chance
(Graham and Piper)
By Emily Conrad

Year 4
Marrying the Billboard Cowboy
(Zeke and Kaitlyn)
By Tara Grace Ericson

Healing the Cowboy
(Clint and Nora)
By Mandi Blake

Year 5
Matchmaking the Cowboy
(Hollis and Lucy)
By Emily Conrad

Caring for the Cowboy's Baby
(Dawson and Liberty)
By Hannah Jo Abbott

Year 6
Doting on His Best Friend
(Milo and Phoebe)
By Liwen Y. Ho

Corralling the Cowboy

(Ethan and Bethany)
By Elle E. Kay

Year 7
Keeping the Cowboy's Promise
(Wyatt and Rachel)
By Hannah Jo Abbott

Fulfilling Her Christmas Wish
(Trevor and Lottie)
By Liwen Y. Ho

Year 8
Playing for Keeps
(Justin and Caroline)
By Mandi Blake

Marrying the Accidental Groom
(Gideon and Juliana)
By Tara Grace Ericson

Year 9
Clearing the Cowboy's Name
(Rowan and Penelope)
By Elle E. Kay

Risking His Heart
(Cody and Neenah)
By Emily Conrad

Heroes of Freedom Ridge Series

Looking for more stories with Christmas, community, and

sweet happily ever afters? Visit Freedom Ridge and discover eighteen more faith-filled stories of Christmas in Colorado.

Join in all the fun at our Facebook Reader Group
www.facebook.com/groups/freedomridgereaders
For sneak peeks, giveaways, and tons of Christmas romance fun!

A sweet small-town romance exclusively for Emily's email subscribers.

Food trailer owner Asher has seen too many tears he couldn't dry. Determined to be part of the solution, he avoids romance and all the heartbreaking drama that comes along with it.

At least, that's the plan until his heart decides it has a mind of its own. If he can't rein it in, he's destined to break not one, but two women's hearts.

Sign up for email newsletters at emilyconradauthor.com and receive *Between The Two of Us*, the prequel novella to the Rhythms of Redemption Romances, as a welcome gift.

Did you enjoy this book?

**Help others discover it by leaving a review on Goodreads
and the site you purchased from!**

Acknowledgments

I have a confession to make. I have very little experience with horses, despite my fascination with them. As you can imagine, this story took research, but a computer only gets a wannabe horsewoman so far. My thanks go out to the ladies who went out of their way to share their experience with me so this story could be as authentic as possible.

Tiffany Noelle Chacon is both a horsewoman and a sweet romance author who graciously read this story and offered feedback grounded in her firsthand experience. Her love and knowledge of horses also flows brilliantly through her own Equestrian Dreams series. Start with her novel *Jump* to follow sisters Mila and Anya Kozak in an equestrian series about facing your fears, falling in love, and building your own happily-ever-after.

Local friends Vicki and Jen also gave me the opportunity to meet Chaz, a real ranching horse who gamely took this very green rider for a little outing. Thank you, ladies, for making the time and answering all my questions!

Jessica J and Jane, thank you for your input on cows!

Jessica J, Amy, and Janet, I appreciate your help polishing up my draft. Danielle, thank you for beta reading. My gratitude also goes out to my editors Brandi and Judy.

Even with all of this help, I'm sure some errors have slipped through. Those are on me.

Readers, it's an honor to get to write stories for you. It's my prayer that Hollis and Lucy's story has added some joy and hope to your life.

Lord Jesus, thank You for hope anchored not in this troubled world but, instead, in You.

About the Author

Emily Conrad writes contemporary Christian romance that explores life's relevant questions. Though she likes to think some of her characters are pretty great, the ultimate hero of her stories (including the one she's living) is Jesus. She lives in Wisconsin with her husband, an energetic coonhound rescue, and two lop-eared bunnies. Learn more about her and her books at emilyconradauthor.com.

 facebook.com/emilyconradauthor

 instagram.com/emilyrconrad